# ELEPHANTS
## IN THE
# DISTANCE

*Also by Daniel Stashower*

**The Adventure of the Ectoplasmic Man**

# ELEPHANTS
# IN THE
# DISTANCE

## Daniel Stashower

William Morrow and Company, Inc.
New York

Library of Congress Cataloging-in-Publication Data

Stashower, Daniel.
Elephants in the distance / Daniel Stashower.
p. cm.
ISBN 0-688-07195-3
I. Title.
PS3569.T33635E44 1989
813'.54—dc19
88-32259
CIP

Printed in the United States of America

First Edition

1 2 3 4 5 6 7 8 9 10

BOOK DESIGN BY NICOLA MAZZELLA

For Fred and Hildegarde

# ELEPHANTS
## IN THE
# DISTANCE

It was nine-year-olds today. Girls mostly, but a few boys. The old magician adjusted his top hat and took a step toward his prop case, chuckling in what he hoped was a grandfatherly way.

"Distinguished guests," the magician said, reaching for a red silk, "with your kind permission, I shall perform now a special trick, one that I have done for many years, for many discerning lovers of magic such as yourselves."

He paused, resting his gloved hand on the lid of a grand piano. He ran his finger along the curve. "Indeed," he said, his voice distant, "not so many years ago my dear wife and I performed this very effect for the Chancellor of Austria himself!" He looked expectantly at his audience, many of whom looked up from their bowls of ice cream.

"The Chancellor was most impressed," the magician continued, "most impressed indeed. Shall I tell you what he said?" In the first row of cross-legged children, the birthday girl took off her paper party hat and plucked at the elastic string, a sign of plunging attentiveness. The magician coughed. "No? Well, perhaps later."

**11**

He peeled off his white gloves and rolled back his French cuffs. "Watch, now! Attend me! I reach into the air, and a coin appears!" He looked hopefully at the birthday girl. Her eyes had lighted on him. "Watch again!" he called, his voice rising slightly. "I shall do it again!" But already the eyes had drifted elsewhere.

Long ago the magician had held audiences rapt as he pulled silver coins from the air with the merest flicker of his fingertips. His hands darted back and forth in the spotlight, then paused, flexed and expectant, savoring the moment as he called the shining coins into being. How the audiences in Austria had loved this effect. The production of money! The miser's dream! Fame came easily then. The grand halls, the Opera House. Finally, a command performance for the Chancellor. How lovely Hilda had looked that night, chattering away as she finished her makeup in the splendid dressing room, teasing him when he lingered a moment too long before the smoky mirrors. He wore a new costume that night, a maroon jacket with leather piping. Never had he felt so presentable, or so confident.

That evening the coins fairly leapt to his fingertips. The sounds of merry astonishment filled the ballroom as he moved among the seated guests, teasing a krone from one man's lapel, coaxing another from an elegant young woman's ear. Hilda trailed behind him with the spun-brass pail, laughing delightedly as he tossed in each new coin, shaking the pail to show its weight.

To see the Chancellor was most gratifying of all. That night it seemed as though, if only for a moment, his heavy burden had been eased. For him the magician saved his grand finale—a flash of fire and a cascade of silver pouring from his downturned hands, clattering across the floor. A smile softened the great man's careworn face. "If only," he had said wearily, "it were so easily done."

That was more than half a century ago. A previous life. Then came the war, America, the unhappiness with Galliard. Now he had to scrape to make a living, and his fingers were not so trustworthy as they once had been. He needed falsehoods to make the coins appear: a moment of cover under a red silk, a dodge behind the beaver hat. Only then would the coins emerge, pinched at the tips of fingers that trembled, if only slightly.

The audience, too, had changed. The world no longer held a place for his type of magic. At best, his thick accent and formal air were pronounced quaint. Magic was no longer a full evening's entertainment, nor did it carry the solemn dignity of fifty years ago. He, who had trod the boards with Blackstone, Kellar, and Thurston, now earned his keep in rumpus rooms and at block parties. He missed the backstage clatter, the drag of the lead makeup spoon across his eyelids as the stately overture swelled from the orchestra pit. He missed the hot lights upon his face. Magicians today were an embarrassment; their costumes seemed little more than sequined underwear, and instead of holding themselves erect in a pleasing and commanding manner, they capered about the stage in a kind of frantic dance.

Yet it was they who prospered while he had to struggle to make himself agreeable, yes, lovable to children who saw far greater miracles each day on television. They sat with their grape-juice lips parted in anticipation, waiting for the next thing, a new thing. At seventy-six, he was not a new thing.

The old magician set his top hat down on his prop case. "My esteemed guests," he said, "I will do something for you now that I know you will enjoy. It is something I do only on the most special of occasions." He dipped into his pocket and withdrew a pencil-thin, uninflated balloon. "What have we here?"

A boy near the coffee table thrust his arm in the air. "I know!" he said, straining forward. "Balloons! Do we each get one? I saw this at the mall! Are you giving them away free?"

"A moment, my young patron." The magician raised

the balloon to his lips and blew, his face reddening with the effort. "And now, I shall tie a knot, make a little twist here, a little fold there—don't be afraid, the balloon will not break—and see? A doggie!"

He held the balloon animal up and pranced it through the air. "Is there anyone here who would like the doggie?" Twenty hands reached out and the air filled with a breathy "Oo! Oo!" sound that signaled urgency.

The magician smiled as if amused. "I will make one for each of you," he said. "All will have a balloon."

This is not magic, he thought as he walked back to his prop case. This is not what I worked all my life to become. Any dolt could fashion these little toys; it is the province of harlequins. Yet this is what the children want—not magic, but something they can take home and play with. Something they can hold over the heads of younger siblings and say, "Look what I got!"

A white swan for the girl in the pink smock. A blue mouse for her bespectacled friend. A green poodle for the boy with braces.

A husky red-haired boy approached. He wore short pants that exposed his scabby knees and a cotton shirt bearing the likeness of a cartoon character the magician did not recognize.

"My name's Special Agent Barnes," he said. "I want a balloon."

"I understood your name to be Tommy," said the magician. "A fine name."

"Nope. Special Agent Barnes," the boy said decisively. "Can you do me a wiener dog? A real long one?"

"A dachshund? Certainly. I will sit down. Then maybe I can make the dachshund." The magician tried to catch his breath. He was too old to be blowing up his own balloons, but the air pump was broken. One or two balloons he could blow up, but not twenty-five. He completed the dachshund and handed it to the boy, who took it with just enough hesitation to show that he was not satisfied. The boy would be back, the magician knew, and soon the first balloons would break against the carpeting and others would come untwisted by rough handling. He would have to make perhaps thirty more balloons.

A girl in white carpenter's garb stood before him. She clasped her hands together, rolled her shoulders forward and swiveled coyly. She would do well in later life. "I want a yellow . . . lion! No! Turtle!"

"Turtle, yes." The magician put his hand to his stomach. There was pain there. He looked down at the balloon in his hands. Its surface glistened with dampness from his palms. He made the turtle slowly, pacing himself. Then a pair of red giraffes for two more children.

Special Agent Barnes returned. "Mr. Sniddler?"

"Schneider," the magician said. "Mr. Schneider."

"I changed my mind," the boy said. "I want a snake."

"A snake I cannot do. A snake has no form."

"Sure it does!" the boy insisted. "You know, a snake. It goes like this!" He spread out his arms. "It's just a long balloon!"

"Very well," said the magician. The room seemed quite hot now, and he continued to have difficulty catching his breath. The pain in his stomach sharpened. What could it be? Lunch? Herring in aspic, a slice of Linzer torte. That couldn't be the trouble.

He would make a cobra. It would be difficult, though, because it required three inflations of the balloon—one to soften the rubber, one to shape the coils, and a third to finish. Again he wished that the air pump had not broken.

"I was going to ask for a monkey," the boy said. "Can you do a monkey?"

The magician inflated a thin red balloon to its entire length, then let the air out against his face. More pain in the stomach, rising now. Slowly, he wound the uninflated balloon around two fingers of his left hand and began to blow again. He had to blow hard, so the balloon would coil around his fingers as it inflated, forming a loose spiral.

There was sweat on his forehead, but he could not release the balloon long enough to mop his brow.

"Monkeys are neat," said the boy. "I saw some monkeys at the zoo. One of them barfed up. Right in front of us. Then you know what he did?"

The room tilted at a sharp angle, then began to spin. The magician stared at the half-inflated balloon wrapped about his fingers. Was this the third inflation, or the second?

"Maybe you could make me a monkey," the boy said "Forget the snake, a monkey's probably easier anyway Red's okay. Do me a red monkey."

"A moment, please," the magician said. He stood up and placed a steadying hand on the edge of his prop case "I am afraid I must rest a moment, I am a bit—" His legs buckled. He fell against the piano, his wrist striking the keys.

"Mr. Sniddler? You okay?" For a moment the old magician's eyes flickered open. He was gratified to see that the face of Special Agent Barnes had gone pale. It occurred to him to say something to the children, so he did, though they would not understand. No matter. He closed his eyes again. A hot shock traveled through his chest.

At least he thought, I did not have to do the red monkey.

# Chapter 1

**W**hen I was eleven, and a great favorite of schoolyard bullies, Schneider was always appearing from nowhere, as if in a puff of smoke. The first time it happened, I was locked in a sweaty half nelson, seconds away from being made to eat dirt. Out of the corner of my eye I saw Schneider's Hudson Hornet pop over the grass shoulder of the playground and smoothly thread its way between the park benches and the swing set. Schneider pulled the car to a stop just a few feet away, so that the radiator grill, hissing and gleaming, loomed over us like a grinning predator. After a moment he tooted his horn with what seemed, under the circumstances, a note of inappropriate gaiety.

"Paul!" he shouted, rolling down his window, "I require an audience with you immediately! Do not tarry with your young chums!" Outgunned, my tormenters reluctantly let me up. I brushed off my pants with perhaps more care than was necessary and hopped into the car without a backward glance.

Once we were safely in the traffic on Broadway, Schneider looked me over as if to gauge that day's unhappiness. "Sour ball?" he offered, gesturing at a paper sack on the front seat. I took one and unwrapped it, then thought to offer him one. "Thank you, no," he said, "I'll content myself with a cigar." We drove on for a while in silence as he cut, warmed, and lit a hideous black panatela, carrying out the entire operation with one hand.

"So," he said, sending a cloud of smoke out the window, "this is fine, is it not?"

"Uh-huh," I said. "Fine."

I knew Schneider only vaguely then. He had been very much in evidence when my father died, stopping by frequently to run errands for my mother. He tipped his hat whenever he caught sight of me on those visits. When he'd left, I'd parade stiff-legged around the apartment, as if possessed by his formal bearing. "Goot day, yunk man," I'd say, tipping an imaginary hat in the mirror.

I squirmed in the seat next to him.

"The weather," he said after a time, "it is warm enough for you?"

"It's fine," I said.

"Goot." He slowed for a traffic light, then changed lanes when the light turned. "Perhaps we should look in on my sister," he said. "I think that would be a fine idea."

"I probably have to go home," I said. "I have all this homework to do. Besides—"

"I think you will like Frieda," he continued, "she runs a pastry shop. A very excellent pastry shop. Perhaps the finest in all of New York City. At this time of the afternoon there are almost always warm cakes that need to be eaten. Are you agreeable?"

I thought it over, telling myself I could hardly refuse a man who had saved me from eating dirt. "Only for a minute," I told him. "And only if I can call home so my mother knows where I am."

"Ah," Schneider said, "I have done so already."

The car swung into an alley and Schneider hopped out, seemingly before we'd stopped rolling. I followed as he rounded a corner and stopped in a doorway. "This is it," he said, sweeping his arm upward at a green awning marked CAFÉ VIENNA. "My sister and I have worked very hard for this place. For her, a life's ambition. For me"—he shrugged—"it was the only means of securing a good cup of coffee in this country."

Schneider pulled me through the door. "Frieda!" he called, "we have had a bad day! The world is unjust! We require a pastry, at once!" He guided me to a corner table. His sister appeared a moment later, bearing a small tray. She was an elegant, powdery woman who smelled of flour and violets. Instantly smitten, I stood up and lifted off my wool ski cap by its tassel.

"I am pleased to see you, young man," she said. Her accent was softer around the edges than her brother's. "Please sit. There is no need for such formality." She set a plate down before me. "I believe you will like this, it is *kirschen kuchen*. Still warm. No pastry for you, Josef. Just coffee. No sugar." She placed a steaming cup on the table. Turning away, she plucked the cigar from her brother's fingers.

I watched her go, then turned to face Schneider, who sat regarding me across the table. He cleared his throat. "I have remarked already, I believe, on the unseasonably warm weather?" I nodded. "Goot," he said. "Very goot." Without further comment he picked up a knife from the table and balanced it on his nose. I stared, my fork poised in midair. A moment later he snatched up the knife, twirled it along his fingertips like a baton, and then swallowed it with a discreet cough.

"How did you—" I began, but he held up a hand for silence. Reaching across the table, he pulled a coin from my ear. Then another, followed by a small live bird. It was more than an hour before I remembered the pastry on the table in front of me. A new way of life had begun.

Schneider started picking me up at school regularly. In the earliest days his intent was to cheer up a spectacularly unpopular boy, nothing more. But over the weeks and months, as my threshold for being cheered rose alarmingly, Schneider grew more ambitious. I became his pupil. To this day, the sleights he taught me remain linked in my mind to the troubles they helped to ease: a back palm when I was chosen last at battle ball, a French drop when my socks were deemed "geeky." One proud afternoon, after a week of Indian rope burns in the locker room, I mastered an especially troublesome dice-stacking effect.

"You take the coin—so!" he'd say. "Bring your arm down—yes! Snap the fingers! *Snap* them! Again!" If I learned the sleight, all was well. If not, he sat back and spoke of what I'd be missing, of the performances that— if only I could master this one subtlety—I would soon be giving for the crowned heads of Europe. A stack of coins stolen from the tails of my cutaway, and a king is dazzled. A swagger stick strapped to my leg for production at the crucial moment, and the heart of a blushing princess is won. I listened with a solemn face, and though at age eleven I seldom wore tails or carried a swagger stick, I understood what Schneider was sharing with me. It seemed of greater interest than blushing princesses.

Within a year we moved our meetings upstairs to Schneider's apartment above the shop. Here the real work began. Originally the room had been a storage area, but over the years, Schneider had converted it into living quarters. A heavy metal door with a crash bar led into the huge open area, cavernous by Manhattan standards, that retained some aspects of the warehouse it had once been— industrial lights tripped at a fuse box, walls of coarse brick and mortar, exposed metal support beams. Tall casement windows, set close to the ceiling to accommodate the storage crates that had once lined the walls, gave a cathedral effect to the room's lighting.

It proved the ideal setting for Schneider's collection of theatrical memorabilia. Framed magic posters covered one wall, representing the best acts of the century—De

Kolta, Kellar, Thurston, Chung Ling Soo, my father. Glass cases held further relics, including a genuine Houdini cuff, a T. Nelson Downs palming coin, and a copper chop cup that had once belonged to Professor Anderson. A vaudeville-era dressing table sat in one corner, its mirror lined with oversize light bulbs.

My favorite feature about "the museum," as I came to call it, was the way in which the equipment from Schneider's old illusion show had been pressed into service as furniture. A heavy pine packing crate he'd once used for escapes and substitutions now served as a coffee table. His Zigzag Cabinet, formerly used to rearrange the head, body and legs of a female assistant, now held his suits and overcoat. He ate his breakfast off the platform of a Floating Lady Illusion. The only nonmagical items in the entire place were a utility sink, a bed, a refrigerator, and a claw-footed bathtub.

Of all Schneider's treasures, none fascinated me more than the fifty-pound traveling prop case in which he carried his light equipment. "Ah! What taste you have, my boy!" Schneider had cried when I first asked about it "What a discerning eye!"

In truth, the thing was hideous, an almost random collection of boards, hinges, wire, and glue suggestive of haste and splinters.

"I made this case with my own two hands," he told me, "from a walnut tree that I chopped down myself, many years ago. Look here." He snapped down the wobbly legs "One minute it is a suitcase, the next it is a table! You do not see work like this, not anywhere. The lid flips over—so!—and we have a perfect working surface! And here'—he pointed to a small silk bag tacked on at the back—"a servanté! What's it for, you ask? My boy, you have much to learn!" He took an orange from a nearby bowl of fruit "See here, let us imagine that this piece of fruit is something our audience must not see." He then palmed the orange so perfectly that not a glimpse was visible—this at a time when I had a struggle to conceal a quarter. "The situation is this: I have completed my effect, with the aid of this unseen piece of apparatus." He flipped his hand palm out and pointed to the orange. "My problem? I must now get rid of it, and quickly! It is like the murder weapons in those books you read. It must be disposed of without the audience seeing. What to do?"

He looked at me expectantly. I shrugged.

"Think! I have just completed a trick, a masterly effect! What will happen?"

I shrugged again.

"Applause, young Paul! There will be applause! And applause is the magician's best friend. In the other artistic pursuits—drama, opera, ballet—the applause is a mere extra, acknowledgment of a job well done. Not so in the sorcerer's trade! Applause is an essential part of the effect. No performance, large or small, is truly complete without it! So, if you will, a hearty round of applause!"

I clapped my hands together in what I hoped was a hearty manner.

"Ah, thank you! Thank you! You are too kind!" He bowed slightly and gave a deferential sweep of his left arm. Then, breaking character, he straightened up and stepped forward, eagerly gripping my shoulders with both hands. "Well?" he asked. "Did you see?" He turned up his empty palms. "The orange is gone! Did you see where it went? Don't look so surprised! It is right here, in the servanté of my wondrous table! How, you ask? Simplicity itself! Watch again."

He resumed his position next to the prop table, this time holding the orange in plain view.

"Now watch: As the gracious audience applauds, the magician looks out at them as if surprised. A becoming blush of modesty steals across his face. He makes a courtly bow, his right hand resting naturally on the tabletop while the left curls gracefully above his head. And—presto! In that split second, while every eye in the house follows the sweeping gesture of the left hand, our devious right hand deposits the orange in the servanté! A simple misdirection! Nearly every effect contains a moment like this—a moment in which the magician must perform a bit of private, unseen magic in order to protect his secrets. Do you see? Good. Now you do it!"

I tried, though at the time I could no more palm an orange than a watermelon, and my best effort to drape my right hand casually on the tabletop was made ridiculous by its height, which was greater than my own.

Even so, I felt privileged even to touch the traveling case, much less to uncover its secrets. In time I came to look on it as some sort of monument to Schneider's past struggles, of which I was then only dimly aware. Later, when I first heard the story of the Jews being cast out of Egypt, I imagined each of them trudging through the desert clutching a bundled infant in one hand and Schneider's prop case in the other.

At the end of each lesson Schneider would clap his hands, clear his throat and pronounce, "You, my boy, you will be a great one!" Then, in a lower tone, more for his own benefit than mine, he would add, "Just like your father."

I have yet to become a great one. In fact, many years passed before I became a working magician at all. But as I shouldered his casket that gray day in March, and later, standing alone at his graveside, there seemed nothing left to do but give one more hearty round of applause. No performance, large or small, is truly complete without it.

# Chapter 2

The first shot was a medium close-up of me putting on a top hat and turning to the camera as I said, "Hi, I'm Paul Galliard." We got it in six takes.

In the second shot I pulled on white gloves, flipped my opera cape over my shoulder and said, "You know, there are times when . . ." Four takes.

Things started to fall apart on the third shot. I was supposed to walk into frame with a housewife bent low over her washing machine. The line was ". . . we all need a bit of magic to get out those persistent dirt, grease, and grass stains."

I kept stumbling over the line. It happens. Last time I had the same trouble with the name of the product— "Stain Begone." I kept saying "Stain Begun" or "Stain Become."

The crew was losing patience. Especially Frankie, the Hungarian cameraman. He had never fully supported the wisdom of the Stain Begone executives, who, for reasons of "spokesman integrity," had insisted on using a real magician in their commercials, rather than an actor playing a magician. The only magic required, though, came at the point in each commercial where I passed my hand over a soiled handkerchief and transformed it into a sparkling white one, thus illustrating the considerable power of Stain Begone. Other than that, it was a question of reading the cue cards and looking reasonably sentient. Both tasks gave me some difficulty.

Terry, the white-bearded director—who at age seventy-seven, still hoped to break into feature films—tried to coach me from up in the booth. Through the glass I could see him leaning into the microphone, drumming his fingers on the console. His voice came from a speaker at the back of the set. "Let's take it again, Paul. Only let's try something a little different. This time, walk to your position, stop, and *then* say the line. Don't try to deliver the line while you're walking. I think that might be what's tripping you up. Sound okay to you?"

I heard soft groans from behind the cameras. "Uh, Terry," I said, my face reddening, "about this walking and talking problem. I can do it. Really. I picked it up in college. Been doing it for—oh—must be seven years now."

"Just try it the other way once, okay? I think it'll be more comfortable for you." He covered the microphone with his hand and whispered something to an assistant.

Cheryl, the actress playing the housewife, as opposed to a real housewife, beckoned me over to the washing machine. "You're hung up on the words," she said gravely. "Don't think in terms of words. Internalize. Let the words become emotions." She often favored us with this sort of information. Earlier she had advised the boom operator to discharge his negative energy.

Terry's voice welled up from the back of the set. "Let's go again, people. Ready any time."

The floor manager leaned in front of the camera, held up the slate and clapped the sticks. I walked, stopped, and blew the line again.

Two takes later Terry changed the wording and I got

through it. The rest of the day went more or less without incident. After seven hours in the studio—not an unreasonable amount of time—we had what we came for: a twenty-eight-second rough cut. A few minor details and we'd be through. Or so we hoped.

At six feet six inches, Wade Judson dominates a room in a way I don't at a mere six four. He'd been a rodeo rider in Arizona until he invented and patented a spray that never failed to get his ridin' duds clean. It pleased the city-slick staff of Reel Thing Studios to make snide comments about Judson's leather boots and bumpkin manner, but I'd found it in my heart to respect a guy who'd built a $22 million business in only eight years.

Through the glass that separated the control room from the shooting floor I could see Judson scowling. That was a bad sign. He alone had the authority to send us home. I took off my gloves, reached into my pocket for a deck of red Aviators, and drifted into the booth doing some casual fans and passes with the cards. I wanted to be on hand when the decision came down. I found an empty chair at the back and sat down to wait.

Judson's scowl deepened as he watched the tape a few times. Technicians began to squirm in their chairs. Out in the studio the floor crew milled about, trying to look like people who'd put in a hard day's work.

Judson sat down at a lighting console and tugged at his bolo tie. He glanced at the director a few times. "Don't know, Terry," he said finally. "Something's wrong. I can't quite put my finger on it, but there's definitely something. Just don't feel right."

Terry swiveled in his chair and took off his headset. "Look, Wade, I know it seems rough now, but it'll look fine once we've adjusted the color and put in the opticals. You'll barely recognize it."

"I know that," Judson said. "That's not what's bothering me. Maybe I'm all wrong, but maybe not. Let's watch it again."

27

I did a dovetail fan with the cards in my hand and then looked up at the monitor bank, a wall of television screens showing assorted blips, color bars, and studio feeds. A high-pitched tone signaled that tape was rolling as a close-up of the chalk slate appeared on several of the screens. A recorded voice came over the speakers, "*Stain Begone, take forty.*" The sticks clapped and there I was, smiling my pleasant little smile.

"*Hi! I'm Paul Galliard.*" The words Famous Magician appeared across my chest. "*You know, there are times when*" —I walked forward as the camera pulled back to show Cheryl in her laundry room—"*we all need a bit of magic to get out those pesky dirt, grease, and grass stains. That's why I recommend—*"

Judson's voice broke in over the recording of mine. "Okay, stop 'er there," he called. "I think I've got it. I think I know what's wrong."

I looked around the booth, a cramped, grim chamber by virtue of the intimidating electronic panels, dim lighting, and sound baffles. The people inside looked equally cramped and grim.

"For one thing, Paul," Judson began, looking back at me, "I wish you wouldn't say 'pesky.' The script, as I recall, says 'persistent.' "

"Sorry."

"And another thing—"

"Look, Wade," Terry broke in, reaching behind him for another tape, "that's not the audio track we were going to use. We have a better one—one where he says 'persistent.' We're going to dub it in with the computer."

"That's right," said a sound technician who may well have had theater tickets for that evening. "We'll patch it in, quick as a—"

"No, that's not the only problem." Judson was standing now, cinching up his hand-tooled leather belt. "It's when he comes walking into the laundry room. I want him to look more—I don't know—a little more concerned."

28

"Concerned?" Terry's face went slack. "I was going for helpful. Helpful and confident. Fatherly, almost."

"Fatherly," I agreed, though that's not high on the list of adjectives I'd use to describe myself. I glanced at the monitors. A frame of me holding up a stained T-shirt was frozen and flickering. I had just passed thirty at the time, and looked younger, despite a lot of gray hair that I've had since my late teens. Helpful and confident, maybe Fatherly? Not even on a good day.

Judson was pacing back and forth in front of the monitor bank now, still hiking up his pants. "We're definitely looking for a—a whudyacallit, a position beyond helpful. We want to be the final authority on spot removal. And above all," he paused, slowing down for emphasis, "we want to show that we care. Could we just try taking it one more time, and slip in a little more concern?"

It was like asking if we could replace the bottom tier of a house of cards. There was no way of smoothing over what we had; it would take a total reshoot.

I suddenly had one of my bright ideas. I tapped the sound man sitting next to me and motioned to borrow his pencil. When he handed it to me, I carefully broke off the tip and wedged it under the nail of my index finger. Then I shoved a book of matches into my pocket and stepped over to Judson.

"Wade," I said, "can I talk to you for a minute?" I looked him straight in the eye, since I was the only one around tall enough to do it. "I think maybe you're being a little hasty. I think we're together on this. If you had to boil the Stain Begone philosophy down to one word, what would it be?"

He rubbed his chin. "Well, I can't say right off—"

"Try. It's a helpful, uh, motivational exercise they do in television work. It gives direction and focus."

"Okay, let's see. One word. Well, 'concern' of course, like I said . . ."

I reached into my tailcoat pocket with my right hand and flipped open the matchbook.

"No," Judson said, "on second thought, 'caring.' That's the Stain Begone philosophy. 'Caring.' Because we care about all the problems faced every day by—"

It took only a second. "You see, Wade? We're thinking exactly alike!" I pulled out the matchbook and handed it to him. "Before we started shooting this morning, at six A.M., I jotted down the one word I thought summed up the aim of the commercial. Open up those matches. See? 'Caring.' Plain as day. And I think all the caring you could want is right there on that tape, if you'll just look at it again."

Judson stared at the matchbook with the word 'caring' scrawled inside the cover. Then he stared at me. A big grin broke over his face. "Paul," he said, "I like you. Always have. But you are the biggest bullshitter I ever saw on two legs." He looked around the control booth. "Listen, folks, I'm sorry. I know what I'm asking, but I also know that I'm paying for it, so we're not leaving until I get what I want." He looked at me again, still grinning. " 'Motivational exercise,' " he said, and left the booth.

Dejected, I sat down again next to the sound man.

"Nice try, buddy," he said, fingering the broken tip of his pencil.

"Yeah, well," I said, "sometimes the magic works, sometimes it doesn't."

As the unwelcome news filtered into the studio, I looked up at the wall of monitors. Most of them showed pictures of me looking insufficiently concerned. Two others featured soap operas in which earnest-looking women advised downtrodden friends to take "one last shot at happiness." On the smallest screen, marked ON AIR, a consumer advocate held up what appeared to be a crepe pan with a flaking Teflon surface. That meant the local news was still broadcasting from an adjoining studio but would be winding up soon. That meant Clara would be coming free.

"Terry, do you need me urgently right now?" I asked.

He shook his head and leaned into the mike. "Reset, everybody. Then half an hour for dinner."

I unwrapped a wilting bunch of violets I'd bought from a street vendor that morning and secured them under my coat with a mitten clip. Then I headed out through the studio, eyes down. I told myself it wasn't my fault we were reshooting, but I felt guilty all the same.

I caught up with her in the hallway that connects the studio and offices of Manhattan Spotlight, the cable news outfit that owns and operates Reel Thing, with the two additional studios that the news people rent out to commercial producers. Clara Bidwell, whose friends back in Atlanta still call her Clara May Bidwell, produces the soft features on the evening edition of *Manhattan Spotlight*. It's mostly the consumer-advocate slot, a few celebrity features, and the occasional tenants' strike. "It's the kind of thing they really go for at Cannes," she says. She's been trying, like everyone else I know in that business, to move into hard news, maybe as an on-camera personality.

She has the looks for it—crow-black hair worn down and long, but somehow untroubled by gravity, smooth skin, high cheekbones, and a good, if slightly pug, nose. The best feature is the eyes. They're a size too big for the rest of her face, with a dove-gray sadness to them.

I found her leaning against a wall in the hallway, paging through a late-edition *Times*. She wore oversize green slacks and a man's blue shirt that draped and curved in an interesting manner. She looked up at me as I approached, top hat in hand, cape billowing behind me.

"Nice outfit," she said. "Bold. Hangs nicely."

"You don't think it's too much? Too East Village?" I

hooked her arm. "Got a minute?" I steered her into the lobby coffee shop.

"Don't tell me," she said, "I'm getting an image . . ." She closed her eyes and arched her palm over her forehead. "I see a grass stain. A large grass stain. A grass stain that will not go away before tonight . . ."

"You're right," I said, "I'm really sorry." We moved to a table by the window, looking out onto Broadway. "We'll have to postpone that hamburger I promised you. We're going to be in the studio through the evening. Until early next year, in fact."

"Hey, that's all right." She patted the back of my hand. "I wouldn't want to stand in the way of artistic expression. Lord knows there are few enough really *good* spot-remover commercials in this life. Far be it from me—"

"I'll make it up to you tomorrow night. A hamburger *and* fries. All the ketchup you want."

"No problem." Clara paused, about to say something else, but she backed off of it as the waitress came over to pour coffee.

I'd known her only four months then, and she made no secret of the fact that our relationship, such as it was, was surviving on a strictly day-to-day basis. It seems I'm frivolous. She sighed. "Don't worry about it," she said.

I coughed for attention and pushed back my sleeves —the universal signal for the start of a magic trick. Clara's eyes failed to light up with anticipation, but I went on anyway. With my left hand I flicked a red silk from my handkerchief pocket and drew it across my upturned right hand a couple of times. Then I spread the silk across my right palm and made sprinkling motions with the fingertips of my left, as though dropping seeds. Slowly—that's the key here, move slowly, you're not hiding anything—I lifted the silk to unveil a hand full of violets. A pretty effect; not easy either. Clara smiled, but grudgingly, as if I had unwittingly proven some kind of point.

"What's the deal here?" I asked. "You women are supposed to love that trick. It said so on the package."

"Sorry." She applauded softly. "Nice trick."

"Problem?"

"Let's not go into it right now."

"Problem?" I repeated, trying to look bright-eyed and attentive. She didn't say anything. I took out my red Aviators and ran through some flourishes. It's a nervous habit. "Look, I'm sorry about dinner, but I did warn you—"

"That's not what's bothering me. That's not it at all."

"What, then?"

She stirred her coffee and set down the spoon. "Do you remember that talk we had last weekend?"

"Last weekend. Gosh, let me see. Let me push aside the veil of time . . ."

"Seriously. When you were getting all defensive about why you do what you do, and you were telling me about your graduate work on that Civil War general? What was his name? Hedgwick?"

"Sedgwick." I said. "Major General John B., 'Uncle John' to his men, 1813 to 1864. Sixth Corps commander. Wounded at Glendale and Antietam. Killed at Spotsylvania. What about him?"

"Well, I couldn't help wondering about old General Sedgwick. I've been thinking about him a lot since then, in fact. There you were, writing a perfectly somber doctoral dissertation on some Civil War general, and then—wham!—you're dressing up in a cape and pulling rabbits out of a top hat. Next thing you know you're hawking spot remover on local TV. How does one go from college professor to TV spokes-magician in one grand sweep?"

"Attrition."

"Seriously. It just doesn't seem natural."

"I see." I leaned back in my chair, buckled the deck and shot the cards from one hand to the other, like a carnival sharpster. "How far the mighty have fallen. Life held so much promise for young Paul. His was to be a blameless academic existence, until one day the siren call of the stage lured him from his study carrel. . . ."

"You'll have to admit, it's a pretty unusual career move. What's the story? That weird business with your father?"

"You're close. Close, but no black panatela. Look, we've been down this unhappy highway a time or two already. I told you before, I'm a man with responsibilities. I have a rabbit, a landlord, and several doves to support. I found myself in need of a real job."

Clara reached across the table and took my top hat—a silk snap-down—off my head. "And I suppose this is a real job?" she asked, trying on the hat. "Your life is just make-believe. Make-believe with a paycheck."

I fanned the cards facedown in a line on the table, nudged a finger at one end and flipped them faceup, Vegas style. "You know," I began, "it's the darnedest thing. There just isn't a whole lot of call for Civil War experts in today's workaday business world. A Boer War expert, sure. Hell, a company like IBM or Xerox will stop at nothing to get their hands on a really good Boer War scholar. They can't get enough of them—MBAs, lawyers, and Boer War experts, they're the ones who command the top salaries today. But the Civil War, for some reason—"

She wasn't listening. She was looking over my shoulder at someone approaching our table. I turned around in my seat. Judson was hurrying over with his kid in tow.

"Paul," Judson called, nodding agreeably at Clara, "I don't mean to bust in on your dinner break, but you'll never guess who dropped by!"

"General John B. Sedgwick," Clara said, to no one in particular.

"You remember my son Josh, don't you?"

In fact I did. I'd met the kid a couple of years earlier, when I first started doing the Stain Begone commercials. I'd spent a long afternoon trying to teach him the subtleties of a 'mystic coin box' he'd sent away for on the back of a cereal box.

"Josh," Judson said, sitting down next to Clara, "Mr. Galliard's father was a very famous magician. Do you remember me telling you that? My daddy took me to see him at the Winter Garden when I was your age. It was a real treat." Judson's wife had recently divorced him, and whenever I saw him, he made noise about needing to spend "quality time" with his son. I think he hoped to impress his ex-wife with the phrase "quality time."

"Josh has become quite a magician since you last saw him," Judson continued. "He has a card trick he wants to show you."

I gestured to the chair next to me. "Have a seat, Josh," I said. "I could use a good card trick right now." The kid was maybe twelve, glum-looking and fat as a whale. He wedged himself into the seat next to me. I looked at Clara, hoping my expression would convey helpless bemusement. She wasn't looking.

"Look, I have to get going now," she said. "I'll talk to you later, Professor. Call me when you get off."

Judson, ever the rough-hewn gentleman, stood up to pull out her chair. I wanted to say something, take her aside to apologize or make plans for later, but young Josh was already struggling so valiantly with a deck of bridge-width Bicycles that I didn't have the heart to leave the table. I gave a foolish little good-bye wave, as if to a departing mailman.

Judson watched Clara go. "Say, Paul," he said, "I'm sorry if I butted in on something here. I didn't mean—"

I shrugged it off and turned to Josh, who had launched into an unusually tedious card-counting effect, roughly akin to sitting through three consecutive renditions of "Ninety-nine Bottles of Beer on the Wall."

"Tell you what, Josh," I stopped him by laying my hand down on the cards. "Why don't you let me run you through some of my tricks. We can work up to that one a little later." I gathered up the deck and showed him a couple of things, a simple card rise, a find-the-aces trick.

He caught on quickly, I'll say that. I even got a couple of laughs out of him. Just as I began to enjoy myself, Terry came looking for me to do some lighting tests in the studio. As I got up to go, the kid looked devastated. I was actually pleased. I thought he was upset because our magic lesson had been cut short. I imagined myself picking him up at school, taking him to the pastry shop, setting him on the road to a magic career. . . .

He cleared his throat. "My dad said you'd make me a balloon," he reported.

Judson grinned, embarrassed. "Josh, maybe if you asked politely—"

"A balloon, huh? I think we can manage that." I fished in my jacket pockets but came up empty. "Tell you what, you walk along with me back to the studio, and we'll see what we can do." We left the coffee shop and headed down the corridor to a janitor's closet where I'd parked Schneider's prop case. I'd been lugging the thing around with me ever since Frieda had given it to me a week earlier, the day after the funeral. I couldn't quite decide what to do with it.

The bag of balloons was sitting on top when I flipped open the lid. I grabbed a handful and twisted a poodle for Josh as we walked back to the Stain Begone set. He seemed particularly pleased with the puffy little tail. I did a giraffe, a swan, and two other breeds of dog while the lights went into position.

"Okay, Paul," Terry said when everything was set, "we're going to take it one more time, from 'We all need a little help getting out those persistent grass stains.' Let's see the concern this time. And some caring. All right, let's have the sticks. . . . Wait a minute. Judy, slap some more makeup on him, he looks pale as a ghost. Okay? Let's go. This is going to be a keeper, I can feel it."

He was wrong. We never got through the take. I saw the red light on the camera. I stepped forward. Then something very much like a flare went off in my head. The convulsions started about the same time.

Much later, when I saw the tape played back, I had reason to be proud of my performance. I'd taken direction well and stayed in character. Even as I crumpled to the floor, with the words "pesky grass stains" dying on my lips, the expression on my face remained very, very concerned.

# Chapter 3

They really do make you ride in a wheelchair when you check out of a hospital. Some kind of insurance regulation. When you're six four, though, riding a wheelchair feels a little like squeezing into a baby stroller. The orderly who gave me my push—I think his name was Ralph—claimed they had a bigger chair but someone had died in it that morning. I told him I'd settle for the smaller one.

"We're gonna miss you in the kid ward, Galliard," he told me, getting a firmer grip on the handles as he eased me down a ramp. "All those tricks you did. I'm thinking that's why the doc kept you an extra day."

I shifted the overnight bag in my lap. "Held over by popular demand," I said. "That's a first. One thing about a bedridden audience, they're grateful for any distraction. I honestly think they'd have watched me tie my shoes with a fair amount of enthusiasm."

We backed through a set of swinging doors and headed for the patient accounts office. "Looks like you got company," he said, nodding toward the far end of the hall. Clara sat reading a magazine. Franklin, her five-year-old son by a previous marriage, busied himself with a pad of construction paper.

"Your kid?" Ralph asked.

"Hers," I said. "But she lets us play together."

Ralph brought the wheelchair to a stop in front of the glassed-in cashier's window. I stood up and started fumbling for my wallet as Ralph deftly spun the chair around and headed away. I still felt a bit wobbly, but that may have been trepidation over paying my bill. My insurance wasn't exactly comprehensive.

The woman behind the glass pushed out a clipboard of forms and carbons. My eye dropped to the bottom line. It was an impressive figure.

Clara hurried over and hooked her hand under my arm. "Don't worry about it," she said. "It's taken care of."

I stared at her blankly.

"Wade Judson took care of it. He made you some kind of Stain Begone employee-at-large. His company insurance will cover the whole thing."

"Just sign," said the woman behind the glass.

"The man's a saint," I said. I scribbled my signature and pushed the clipboard back under the glass.

"You should have seen him after your—your episode," she said. "He thought he'd killed you, and he knew he was liable. I've never seen so much sweat pooling on one upper lip. He practically fell over himself to assume the expense."

"I'm willing to let him," I said. "I'm generous that way."

Clara led me over to the waiting area, clutching my arm as though I might collapse again at any moment. Franklin sat cross-legged in a hard plastic chair, putting the finishing touches on a drawing.

"Franklin," I said. "You're looking well. It's a delight to see you again. How's the lumbago?"

"Do you get to go home now?" he asked. "Are you done being sick?"

"For the moment," I said.

He held up his construction pad. "I made this," he said, holding up a drawing of a tall purple stick figure wearing a top hat. "See that?" Franklin pointed to the figure's head. "He has a thernometer. Because he's sick."

"This is lovely," I said. "I must have it for my refrigerator door. The big empty head is particularly effective. Trade you for an ice cream cone?"

Franklin nodded.

"We'll have to get that later," Clara said. "Right now we're taking Paul home." She took Franklin's hand and led us both through the automatic exit doors.

It was an overcast morning, but it felt good to get outside after two days. I slung the strap of my overnight bag over my shoulder, refusing Clara's offer to carry it for me.

"I tried to borrow my sister's car," Clara said, "but she needed it. We'll have to grab a cab."

"Let's just walk," I said. "It's only a few blocks."

"You sure you're up to it? You don't look all that well. You look like hell, actually."

I took Franklin's hand and started down Amsterdam. "I can truthfully say I've felt worse."

"When? When have you felt worse?"

"In college. Something to do with midterms and diet pills. It's all kind of a blur now." Clara looked over at me, alarmed. "Just kidding," I said.

"Seriously, what happened to you? Did they ever figure it out? I saw them carry you out of the studio. You were twitching and mumbling something about rebel cavalry. They say you were delirious for three hours, but nobody could find a cause."

"It's a real puzzler," I said. "Franklin, do you know what that says?" He had paused to peer into a newspaper vending machine. "It says 'Small Boy Looks into News Box.'"

"It does not," he said.

"You looked fine when I left you at Reel Thing," Clara

continued. "A little overdressed, maybe, but basically healthy."

"They're still waiting on a few test results. I really don't think it's anything to worry about, I feel fine now. Listen, speaking of Reel Thing, do you mind if we hop a bus and go down there for a second? I left Schneider's traveling case there and I want to grab it before somebody divines its mystic secrets."

"Forget it," Clara said. "I'm taking you straight home. I'm sure your little magic kit will keep until tomorrow."

"If you're going back down there, maybe you could pick it up for me. I think I have a show coming up to-day or tomorrow. A birthday party. I need to check my calendar."

We stopped at a corner and Clara gave me a hard look. "What is it with you? Can't you stop doing magic tricks for a minute? Why are you so fixated on that stupid crate of stupid magic tricks? I think the psychiatrist at the hospital was right—you recently lost the only father figure you've ever had and now—"

I stopped walking. Then I scooped Franklin up off the sidewalk and carried him over to a pretzel vendor. "What psychiatrist are we talking about here?" I asked when Clara came up behind me.

"The one at the hospital. He said that you—"

"Back up a minute. A psychiatrist examined me at the hospital? Was I even awake?" I set Franklin down and handed him a pretzel with yellow mustard. "Take small bites and chew slowly, using this napkin often. This'll help you quit the cigarettes."

"Thank you," he said.

"It was more of a consult, really. I think he was a friend of your intern. He just came in and offered an opinion."

"Based on what? Based on my prostrate form? Based on my life history as related by a woman I've known only four months? That inspires a whole lot of confidence, let me—"

42

"Frieda Schneider was there too. Apparently she'd told him the whole story. The thing about your father."

I started walking again. We happened to be passing the library where I'd logged a lot of hours on my unfinished dissertation. "It's best," I told Franklin, "not to place one's entire faith in modern psychiatry."

"Uh-huh," he said. He had stopped again, to examine the window of an electronics shop. Several televisions were going, and there was an old Stain Begone commercial on one of the channels. Franklin pointed at it. "If you're on the TV, how can you be here?"

"Magic," I said.

"Video tape," Clara corrected. "Look, Galliard, before we get all defensive, let's take stock here for a minute. The psychiatrist didn't analyze you, obviously. He only suggested that what happened to you *might* have had something to do with Schneider's heart attack."

"Really," I said evenly. "What a splendid insight. I'm stunned. Give me a minute to take it in." I stroked my chin. "Yes, it's all clear now."

"Well, they didn't find anything *medically* wrong with you. Do you have any better ideas?"

"I do have something like an idea, actually. I want to check something out in Schneider's prop case."

"Not today. I'm taking you home. Your props and your obsessions will keep until tomorrow." She led Franklin away from the shop window.

"Probably," I said, falling in alongside. "Want to have dinner later? I still owe you."

"You sure you're feeling all right?"

"I have kind of a sore throat. Can you recommend a really good psychiatrist?"

"We'll have to make dinner on the late side. We're putting a segment together for the late edition. The comeback of the hoop skirt. I have to ride herd over the production assistants. I'll come by when I'm through."

"And Franklin? He's welcome to join us, actually."

"I'll leave him with my sister and be at your place by ten, with any luck. And a tail wind."

"Mind if we make it your place?"

"Why?"

"Why, indeed? A good question."

I wanted to make it her place because I knew there was going to be a stupid crateful of stupid magic tricks scattered all over my apartment by evening, but I didn't think it prudent to say so. "Let's consider," I said. "You have a palatial Murray Hill co-op, working fireplace, working stereo; I have a slime-pit efficiency on 104th, barred windows, odor of rabbits. Both places have their charms, but—"

"All right, but promise me you'll get some rest?"

"Unless I have a show this afternoon."

"Of course. Silly of me to think of your health. The show must go on."

The two of them dropped me at the corner of Amsterdam and 104th and waited until I got through the door of my apartment. I waved them off and began unlocking my mailbox. I waited a few minutes, pushed the letters back into the box, and headed for the subway.

My collapse in the studio had me worried for a couple of reasons. It wasn't the first time I'd fallen flat on my face by any means. I had been, in my day, a heroic drinker. That hadn't been a factor this time, though. It had been perfectly clear to me the minute I woke up in the hospital: I had blown up some balloons and wound up on my back. Schneider had blown up some balloons and wound up in the morgue. The balloons I'd used came from Schneider's traveling case. Even without a Ph.D., I sensed a connection.

As usual, the red-line local got stuck between the Sixty-sixth and Fifty-ninth street stations. That gave me ample time and a pleasant setting to ponder the absurdity of what I was thinking. Old men have heart attacks all the time, I told myself. Was it really necessary to find conspiracies lurking behind natural events? He'd kicked off. I hated it, I'd be a long time getting over it, but it had happened.

So what the hell had happened to me? Could it really have been a sympathy seizure, something psychosomatic? I didn't like to think so, and yet there'd been no abnormalities in my system. Or none that had shown up in the blood screen.

The subway got moving again after about twenty minutes, and I completed the trip to Reel Thing without further delay. I knew Clara was likely to turn up there sooner or later, so I went in through a side door and didn't talk to anyone. The traveling case was in the janitor's closet where I'd left it. I spent another half hour wrestling it onto a crowded subway car in the first wave of rush hour. By the time I'd lugged it up the three flights to my apartment, I was so out of breath that I began to revise my thinking; if Schneider really had died of a heart attack, I wouldn't begrudge him.

I set the case down inside the door of my small, small apartment. I didn't open it right away. I knew I was about to cross some sort of line, and I didn't especially want to.

My roommate had been out of town for over a week, so I spent a few minutes checking the food and water supply for my rabbit and doves. Then I played back the messages on our answering machine; two from my roommate's mother, one from Frieda, and one from a perky-sounding woman named Mindy Kramer, who wanted to talk to me about a television special she was helping to produce.

I looked again at the prop case, but decided instead to sort through my mail. Nothing much there except the latest issue of *Genii* magazine, with a cover story on Yen Soo Kim, "the Asian Astonisher." I flipped through the pages to an article on "the exciting new pull-vanishes." This failed to hold my attention for very long. I looked around for some plants to water, but my roommate had killed them all since I last checked.

The balloon pump was sitting on top of the pile of equipment when I finally opened Schneider's case. It was a patchwork job that he'd put together himself, like all the rest of his apparatus. The pump had three parts, an accordion bellows that fed into a narrow three-foot length of flexible tubing, with a tip at the end that fit into the nozzles of balloons. Schneider carried the pump over his shoulder with a leather strap when he was doing a strolling show, and set it down on the ground to work the bellows with his foot when he was ready to twist balloons. It was a serviceable piece of equipment. He'd used it for more than twenty years.

I placed the bellows on the floor and stepped. It didn't compress. I stepped harder, pulling on the tube to free up any kinks. Still nothing. I stomped on the bellows with all my weight and the tube popped off. I picked it up off the floor and tried blowing through it. There seemed to be some kind of blockage, so I laid the tube on the kitchen counter and slit it up the side with my Swiss army knife. Halfway up, the knife got stuck on a clot of something hard and gray.

I didn't know what the clot was or how it had gotten into Schneider's balloon pump. It seemed reasonable to assume that Schneider had not put it there himself. Nor did it seem likely that it had lodged there of its own accord.

Someone must have clogged up the old magician's balloon pump, and the result was clear enough. With his pump out of service, Schneider would have to blow up his own balloons the next time he did a show.

I took a handful of balloons from the case. They were good ones—the two-sixty length, fairly fresh. I sniffed at the nozzles. They smelled bad. They always smelled bad, but this was different. I looked over at the dismembered pump, then back at the balloons. I, for one, wasn't about to blow them up.

# Chapter 4

I arrived at Research Lab D just as Erica sliced into a fetal pig. "Darling!" she cried as I came in. "Just the man I need to see! Look at this." She pointed to a bloodstain on the lapel of her lab coat. "It won't come out, no matter what I do. Think you can put the fix in at Stain Begone? Maybe get me a commercial of my own?"

Erica is part of a network of professional student friends left over from my days in the History Department. I consult with them every once in a while, just to keep my hand in. A friend in Asian Studies helped me put together some patter for a new Chinese Rice Bowls routine—probably more authentic than strictly necessary. Another friend in veterinary medicine figured a way to get my doves to come when I clap. Erica had been in med school for what seems like forever. Since Eisenhower's day, she likes to tell people.

"How are you feeling?" she asked, enjoying my visible discomfort as she pinned back flaps of pigskin. "Are you done having psychotic incidents on film?"

"It was nothing of the kind," I said. "I had a psychotic incident on *tape*. How did you hear about that?"

"We're a pretty gossipy bunch in the medical community." She looked down at the pig. "So," she said into its open stomach, "still won't talk, eh?" She lifted out a brownish mass.

"I don't suppose you feel like taking a break, huh?"

"Can't. Anyway, are you all right now? I assume that's what you came to see me about."

"More or less. Look, Erica, this is going to sound weird . . ."

"Weird? From you? Heaven forfend!" She looked down at the pig again. "I could tell you stories about our friend Paul that would curl your tail."

"Erica. Stay with me here. Do you still know anything about toxicology?"

"A thing or two, yes."

I took a handful of balloons from my pocket and spread them out on the lab table. "Think you could test these? For poison?"

"You're kidding, right?"

"No, I'm not kidding. I don't think so, anyway."

Erica pulled off her rubber gloves and led me away from the dissecting pan with her arm around my shoulders. "Darling," she said, "don't take this wrong. I say this only because I love you. You've gone crazy. Seek help." An Erlenmeyer flask filled with tea sat brewing on a Bunsen burner. She poured two beakers full and handed one to me.

"Remember that delightfully shy, studious young man I used to know? Remember how he'd stay up until all hours grappling with grave historical problems, his scholar's brow furrowed in thought? Remember what a splendid fellow he was?" She gave a theatrical sigh. "Whatever happened to that guy?"

"Tell you what. Why don't you run the test in his memory?"

"Get serious, darling! You really think someone's trying to poison you?"

"Not me. A friend of mine. If I'm right, I just got hold of the poison by mistake." I put my hands on her shoulders. "I'm absolutely serious about this. Do the test. For old time's sake." I fluttered my eyelashes. "Please."

She sighed. "I'll call you when I know," she said. "You'll forgive me if I don't rush right to it." She turned back to the lab table. "Miss me?" she asked the pig.


A Friday rush-hour rain was falling when I got outside. I took refuge in an automatic bank-teller alcove and unfolded a page I'd torn from Schneider's date book. There was no point in trying to flag a cab in the rain, so I charted my best course on the bus.

My chartings were a little off, so it took me a while to find the right address. By that time the rain was coming down harder. The apartment complex, which was done up in somebody's idea of Tudor, had about seven entrances, all quaintly hidden. I found the right doorway by the dim light of flame-shaped bulbs fitted into hurricane lamps. Inside the lobby stood a creaky buzzer panel that may also have been from the Tudor period. The markings had long been scratched off, so I picked a button that seemed, through a sort of loose geometry, to correspond with the apartment number marked on the page of Schneider's date book.

A small apartment crammed with large furniture means one of two things to a magician—an elderly couple entertaining a visiting grandchild, or a recently divorced mother easing her child over the first birthday. The woman in the doorway seemed to fit the latter category. She had a "rising young partner" look: about five six, gray wool suit, royal-blue silk blouse and floppy bow, Reeboks. A wet raincoat hung over a chair in the short entryway, along with a thin pebbled-leather artist's portfolio. She wore her light brown hair in a layered, studiously casual look I've heard called "big hair."

"Miss Rawlins?" I asked.

She nodded.

"I appreciate your seeing me."

She nodded again and waved me to a chair. "Drink?" she asked.

I wanted one, but said no for good form.

She shrugged and took down a glass from a huge pine breakfront. "When you called," she began, "I really didn't know what to say. I'm not sure how I can help you. This whole thing has been so unpleasant—"

"I know," I said quickly, "and I'll try to be as brief as possible. If you could just tell me, Miss Rawlins—"

"Jane," she said, pouring a lot of Scotch and a little water over ice. "You may as well call me Jane."

"If you could just tell me, Jane, whatever you can remember about that day, it would help me a lot. I need to find out as much as I can."

She cocked her head as if trying to remember something. "What's your interest in this? I can't remember what you said on the phone."

"The man who died in your living room was my uncle," I lied. "My only relative."

"Oh. I'm sorry." She offered me a cigarette, which I had less trouble refusing. Then she sat down near a coaster and an ashtray and motioned me to the chair opposite. "I'm not sure exactly what I can tell you apart from the obvious, and I already told that to the police and the man from the coroner's office."

"Anything would be helpful," I ventured.

She sent up a cloud of smoke. "Truth of the matter is, I wasn't even in the room when your uncle had his attack. That's what was so terrible about it. I was in the kitchen scooping ice cream, if you can believe it. I have a—I'm seeing someone, and he was supposed to be in the room with the kids, but he'd slipped into the other room to catch a few minutes of the game. . . ." She gave me a boys-will-be-boys look. "Then all of a sudden I heard shouting, and my daughter came running in—"

"Do you suppose I might talk to her?" I asked.

Jane stiffened in her chair. "No," she said firmly. "Alexandra's not—she's not home yet, and I don't want her dragged into this anymore. This whole experience has been horrible for her. She doesn't show it much now, but you never know how deeply these things run—"

I sat forward on the edge of my chair. "I'll promise not to upset her," I said. "I work with children every day. If I could just wait until she comes home—"

"Mr. Galliard, I'm sorry about your uncle. Truly. But I can't allow—" She broke off as if suddenly embarrassed. Her eyes fixed behind me.

"You're the guy from TV," said a voice.

"Alexandra, I *asked* you to stay in your room until—"

I swiveled in my chair to face a pale nine-year-old girl wearing an oversize fatigue jacket. Behind her an open door led into a small room illuminated by the glow of a television set.

"You're on the commercial," she continued, blithely ignoring her mother. "You're the guy who makes the spots float out over the shirt and go like that." She waved her arms as if magically dispersing an especially tenacious grease stain. "They do it 'cause of cameras and trapdoors, right?"

"Alexandra, I *asked* you—"

"Trapdoors?" I said. "Alexandra, you wound me." I reached into my jacket pocket. "I have a trick here I think you'll like. It won't help you with your dirt, grease, and grass stains, but it does involve soap. Like to see it?"

"Paul—Mr. Galliard—I really don't think this is appropriate. And Alexandra, I did ask you—"

"Mother," the girl said with heavy exasperation, "he's from *TV*."

Jane wavered. I felt bad for putting her on the spot, but not too bad. She hesitated a moment and then made for the liquor cabinet, giving a little sigh of resignation.

Alexandra returned her attention to me.

"Do you know what this is?" I asked.

**51**

"Sure. It's a soap-bubble thing. Wand. You get them in soap bubbles."

"Do you have any soap bubbles?"

"No. I used to, but they spilled."

"Well, hang on a minute . . ." I dipped the wand into the breast pocket of my jacket. I have a plastic Ziploc bag tacked in there. That's where I carry my bubble liquid. It always gets a laugh out of adults; kids seem to think it's a good idea.

I dipped the wand twice and blew a bubble. "All right, watch this. You see that bubble there? I close my fist around it, and violà! The bubble disappears!"

"Oh, *great*." Heavy exasperation again. She did it quite well. "Real great. Anybody could do that."

I registered disappointment. "Really? Anybody? Well, let's try again anyway." I dipped the wand with my right hand while my left stole into a trouser pocket to palm a hollow, clear plastic ball. "Okay. Watch again. And wipe that disgusted look off your face. I blow the bubble, close my fist around it, and—hey, wait a minute." I stared at the clear plastic ball in my hand. "That's weird. The bubble didn't disappear that time."

Now she was hooked. I kept the talk fairly neutral as I ran through some standard touch-palms, French drops, and fist-vanishes with the clear plastic ball. As I launched into a multiplying soap bubbles routine, one I'm particularly proud of, I began maneuvering toward Schneider.

"You like magic, don't you, Alexandra?" I asked. Holding one plastic soap bubble between my thumb and forefinger, I dipped the wand back into my pocket and blew a stream of bubbles toward my left hand. Now there were two balls clipped between my fingers.

"Pretty much," she allowed.

"Do you see a lot of magic on TV?" I repeated the move. Three balls.

"Yeah, and there was a guy here at our house. For my birthday. But he got sick in the middle of it and had to go home."

I looked over Alexandra's shoulder at her mother, guessing by her worried expression that she hadn't told her daughter of Schneider's death.

"He's much better now," I said, waving my hand aloft. Now there were four balls spaced between my fingers. That's usually the end of the routine, but I'd rigged up a little kicker. "He asked me to say hello. He'd have come himself, but he had football practice."

"Is he on TV like you?"

I held up the four soap bubbles in my left hand and slapped them against the palm of my right. Now I had eight bubbles—four in each hand. It took me seven months to figure out a way of doing that. "He would be, only he keeps getting sick all the time. None of us can figure it out."

"Yeah," she said, still watching my hands. "That's weird."

"None of us can figure it out at all," I repeated. "Sometimes he's giving a magic show and everything will be going along as usual"—I began to vanish the balls, one by one —"and then the next minute he's hanging from the chandelier and juggling watermelons. But hey, what am I telling you this for, you've seen it already."

"No, I haven't," she said, her eyes going wide. "He didn't do that."

"No? No chandelier? No watermelons? Then I suppose he did his other little stunt, where he paints the room blue while a camel recites the Gettysburg Address."

"Nuh-*uh*," Alexandra said. "That's not what happened."

"No? Boy, this is a real puzzler." I vanished the last of the plastic balls and clapped my hands together once. "Well, was it the thing with the balloons?"

She nodded, but didn't elaborate.

"The thing where he *pretends* he's going to make some balloon animals, and then he does maybe one or two of them, stops, blows a whistle, and a long line of penguins comes marching into the living room?"

"Nuh-*uh*," she repeated.

"I don't believe there was a magician here at all," I said. I stood up and started putting on my coat. "I think you're just taking cruel advantage of my good nature."

"Was too!" Alexandra cried. "There was, too, a magician here! He was right here!"

"Did he blow up balloons?" I asked.

"Yeah."

"Did the marching penguins come in?"

"No. He just made the balloons."

I paused. I felt Jane trying to catch my eye, but I kept my attention fixed on Alexandra. "Just the balloons? Nothing else?"

"He was standing right here, and he started blowing them up. I got a red giraffe."

"That's my favorite," I said.

"I wanted green," she said. "A green giraffe. But before I could go back he gets this weird face ,." She screwed up her features. "And he grabs his arm like this . . ." She clawed at her right shoulder. "And then he falls over like this . . ." She sprawled acrobatically across the sofa and lay there with her eyes closed.

After a moment she opened them. "It was real scary," she said. "Tommy Barnes said he'd be too scared to sleep that night, but he didn't bring a present, so I didn't care."

"Alexandra, really," said Jane, but her daughter was now too deeply involved in her story to take any notice.

"I ran over and asked if I could help, if I could get him some water or an aspirin, but he just kept talking."

I waited for her to go on. When she didn't, I prompted. "Did he want water?" I asked.

"No, he kept talking about balloons. He kept saying, 'Red cats, red cats,' which was weird 'cause of he was supposed to be making a red monkey, even though what I wanted was a green giraffe."

"Red cats?"

"Yeah, and he kept grabbing at his arm and making this face." She got up and made to repeat the performance.

54

"I think that's enough, don't you, Paul?" Jane took a step forward and put her hands on her daughter's shoulders.

I stood up. "Uh, certainly. I guess that ought to do it, just about. I want to thank you for all your help." I bent down and extended my hand. "Thank you, Arnold."

"My name's not Arnold!"

"Oh. Sorry, Ted." I shook her hand gravely and headed for the door. Jane said something polite about how nice it was to have met me.

I said, "Could I possibly take you up on that drink offer now? I suddenly feel as if I could use it."

Two drinks later I headed for the street, leaving a green giraffe propped against the apartment door. The rain was still falling as I made my way to the bus stop. From the street I could see Alexandra staring down at me from a third-floor window, clutching her shoulder and contorting her face.

Like Tommy Barnes, I would not be able to sleep that night.

# Chapter 5

Erica was sitting cross-legged on the doorstoop of my apartment when I returned. She scrambled to her feet when she saw me coming, folding up a blue travel umbrella.

"Well," I said. "This is most unexpected."

"I try to keep you on your toes, dearest," she said. "My other pleasures are so few." There was a brittle anxiety in her voice, despite the jokey tone. "Well? Invite a girl in out of the rain?"

"Please." I held the outer door for her.

"I tried calling, but I got the damned machine. I thought I'd try to catch you on my way home. Or Michael." She swept past me and struck a dramatic pose in the alcove, slumped against a tile wall, delivered from the rain. "Where is your roommate, anyway?"

"Manassas. A reenactment. Then a dealers' convention in Herndon, Virginia."

Erica gave a distracted nod and chewed at her lower lip. "Darling," she said. "I have news." She reached into the pocket of her yellow rain slicker and withdrew a clear plastic bag. Inside were the brightly colored animal balloons I'd given her that afternoon. She held the bag at arm's length, pinched between her thumb and forefinger. "We've had quite a time together, these balloons and I."

I unlocked the inner lobby door and led her up the stairs. "I take it you discovered something on the nozzles?" I fumbled with the three locks on my apartment door. "Something apart from my saliva?"

Erica nodded, but didn't say anything more. I got the door open and again she swept past me, this time to fling herself at a wingback chair. She gave no sign of being ready to reveal anything, and I knew better than to try rushing her.

"Tea?" I asked.

"If it's not too much trouble."

I made my way to the kitchen—a wondrously short distance from the door, bathroom, and everything else in the apartment—and set a pan of water on the stove. Erica had her coat off and a cigarette going by the time I came back into the room.

"Paul," she said, "when you came to me this afternoon, I really didn't expect—"

"I know."

"I mean it's really—"

I cut her short. "What did you find?"

She tossed me the plastic bag, or tried to. It flopped to the floor at my feet. "You may have a tough time believing this, but there was definitely something strange there. I think it was isoproterenol."

"Isoproterenol! I suspected as much!" I smacked my fist into my hand. Erica took a slow drag on her cigarette and narrowed her eyes at me. "Okay," I said, "what is isoproterenol?"

"It's a drug to relieve bronchial spasms, a fairly common one. Did your friend have bronchitis? Something he might have used a prescription drug for?"

"Not that I know of."

"If he did, I'd have advised him to change pharmacists.

The dose looked a little strong. The stuff is supposed to be diluted in a water solution; this wasn't. I did a little reading. Isoproterenol contains a cardiac stimulant, so naturally it's not given to anyone with any kind of heart condition. In a normal dose it can cause all kinds of problems. In this form . . ." She let her voice trail off. "How many of those balloons did you blow up?"

"Five or six."

"That would more than account for your seizure."

I sat down heavily on the edge of the sofa bed. After a couple of minutes I heard the water boiling in the kitchen. This time it took me longer to cover the distance. When I returned with the tea, my hands were shaking. I notice things like that. It's why I cut back on coffee.

I handed Erica her tea and sat down with mine. "There's something else that will interest our friends at the police department," she said. "You are going to the police, aren't you?"

"Hadn't thought about it. I guess so. Of course."

"They'll want to know this. The stuff was introduced in a medium of DSMO."

I looked up expectantly, but she just took a sip of tea. If I wanted to know, I'd have to ask.

"What's DSMO?" I said dutifully.

"It's a penetrant. It allows medication to travel through the skin into the bloodstream. No shots, no pills. You know those motion-sickness ear patches people wear nowadays? That's DSMO. The medicine penetrates the sensitive skin behind the ear."

"And you found it on the balloons, along with the isoproterenol?"

"I think so. It would account for the garlicky smell, but our equipment isn't exactly—"

"Tell me something. If this DSMO penetrates the skin so readily, were the kids at the birthday party at any risk?"

She thought about it. "Not especially, I guess. Not unless they had heart conditions. And you'd have had to

59

have handled more than one balloon to get the cumulative effect of this stuff. Besides, the isoproterenol was all on the nozzles. Only the person who inflated the balloons would be exposed, really."

"Sounds very clinical. Very well thought out."

"I suppose," she said.

"Not the sort of thing that would happen by accident."

"Hardly."

"It also sounds as if someone hedged his bets. Left nothing to chance." I set down my cup and walked over to the window, which looked out on a broad expanse of brick and a cluster of trash Dumpsters. "Careful planning. That's a quality much prized in the magic community."

Erica lit another cigarette and watched the smoke from the spent match curl into the air. "What do you mean 'hedged his bets'?" she asked.

I told her about the clogged air pump. "Suppose Schneider had been able to fix the pump," I said. "Let's suppose he found the clog and replaced the hose; it's not that unlikely an occurrence, now that I think of it. He was pretty careful with his apparatus. But even if he had been able to fix the pump and hadn't had to blow up the balloons with his mouth, he'd have still died."

Erica didn't look so sure. "Possibly," she said. "Assuming, of course, that it really was the isoproterenol that killed him. You're going to need a real medical examiner to help you there. But if he—or you, for that matter—hadn't had to touch the nozzles of the balloons to his lips, there'd still have been some effect. The drug would have crept in through his fingers. Maybe it would have killed him. It sure would have taken longer."

I didn't say anything. After a while Erica came over and sat next to me on the sofa bed. "Look, darling," she said, draping her arm around my shoulders, "I don't know exactly what it is you've gotten yourself into here, but I can't think of anyone more ill-suited to handle it. No offense, but if I were murdered, you're the last person I'd want tracking down the killer. You lack a certain ruth-lessness. You're more of a Boy Scout. A big-brother type. Good Lord, you actually are a Big Brother."

"I've always seen myself as more of a steely-eyed man of action."

"Right. Well, that's part of your considerable charm. Don't get me wrong, poppet, I love you dearly. But you're a nice guy. Too nice to get any notions about bringing your dear mentor's killer to justice. I just can't see it. Go straight to the police."

I nodded slowly as Erica hopped up and pulled on her rain slicker. "I must go now," she said. "The lab crea-tures get restless when I'm away too long." I followed her to the door. "Still seeing that person from the television studio?" she asked, too casually. "The ugly one saddled with the child? What was her name?"

"Clara," I said.

"Is it true love? Do you find her intoxicating?"

"I'm interested. Very. She seems to have some sus-picions about me, though."

Erica reached up and grabbed my shirt collar. Then she pulled my face down close to hers. "Give her my very best, won't you?"


After Erica left, I went trawling in my laundry hamper for a passably clean shirt to wear to work that night. Then I exchanged my corduroy sport coat, the one with the soap-bubble pocket, for a navy wool blazer that I wear for close-up work. This one has a coin dropper pinned into the back vent and a rising-card effect sewn into the handkerchief pocket. I didn't have time to shave, but I did select a new tie from my luxurious collection of four—this one a ma-roon silk with blue and gold paisleys. I threw some cards, rope, and sponge balls into a small leather briefcase and left my apartment at about seven-fifteen.

I have unofficial magician-in-residence status at a bar

called Hugo's on Columbus and Eighty-third. It's a neighborhood hangout, one that looked the other way when ferns and brass railings came through, and has so far managed to hold the line against granite tables and black walls. I work anywhere from two to six hours behind the bar on weeknights, eight hours on Saturday nights. Mostly I do bar stunts and sucker bets; stuff involving coins under shot glasses and bills in lemons. The aim is to keep the bar stoolers entertained enough so that they'll laugh, nudge each other's ribs, and order more drinks. Once in a while I get to do the odd trick that requires a modicum of skill.

That night I decided to walk rather than catch a bus. I had, to put it mildly, a lot to think about. At least Erica's lab tests proved that Schneider's death had been no ordinary heart attack, I thought as I walked along. That meant that what I'd suffered had been no panty-waist psychosomatic fainting spell, by God. No sir, we were talking murder. I wondered if I was supposed to feel better or worse in that knowledge.

Business was slow at the bar, so I pulled a short shift that night, knocking off at about nine-thirty. I still wasn't quite done with my dark night of the soul concerning Schneider's death, so I decided to walk and brood my way back to my apartment before keeping my late dinner date with Clara. I also thought I'd get a shave in, for good measure.

The phone began ringing as I climbed the steps to my apartment. I thought I'd turned on the answering machine, but on the third ring I realized I hadn't. I set my briefcase down in the hall and scrambled with the door locks. Naturally I had trouble with the keys. I threw the door open on the fifth ring and hurried inside.

The flash was bright orange. It looked like a gunfire spurt against the blackness, but there was no sound except a low crackling noise. Then I saw the flames.

I turned and ran for an extinguisher in the hall, tripping at full speed over the briefcase I'd left outside the door. That sent me sprawling down the flight of stairs to the lobby. I didn't really hurt myself until I got to the bottom and slammed my head against the tile floor. That hurt. Quite a lot. As I blacked out, for the second time that week, my thoughts scattered slowly. The last to go were those about big red cats and little green balloons.

# Chapter 6

There were 255 acoustical tiles on the ceiling of Lieutenant Chasfield's office. I'd had time to count them twice. Each tile had forty-nine holes in it, for a grand total of 12,495 holes. I'd had to work that one out on paper. Finished with the higher math, I shifted again on my steel folding chair and pressed the chemical cold pack I'd been given to the back of my head. Then I went back to wondering where I'd heard the name Chasfield before.

The previous night had not been a good one. The fall down the apartment stairs was the least of it. I'd given my head a pretty resolute crack, but it had only knocked me out for a few seconds, so far as I knew. As soon as I came to, I hauled myself back up the stairs with the noble idea of charging into my burning apartment to pull my frightened, pink-eyed rabbit to safety. It hadn't been necessary; things weren't that bad. The place was full of smoke, and there were a few small fires burning on the carpet and one in the seat of my wingback chair, but nothing a former cub scout couldn't handle. The extinguisher in the hallway didn't work, I discovered, but I'd managed to smother the smaller fires with the bath mat. It was pretty much over by the time the fire department arrived. The only things destroyed were the chair, a rug, my telephone and answering machine, a small footstool, a potted palm that was already dead from neglect, my back issues of *Genii* magazine, and Schneider's traveling case.

It was this last item that had really caught my attention, as I'd tried to explain to the firemen and to the two police officers who showed up a scant half hour later. They weren't much interested in Schneider's traveling case. The policemen spent a lot of time asking me questions about gas heat and cooking safety, while the firemen tramped around 'securing' the place. As near as I could figure, securing the place meant fingering my roommate's collection of Civil War figurines and opening and closing the refrigerator door a few times.

My landlord also had a fair number of questions to ask me, but his centered on how soon I could get my careless behind out of his building. He didn't much care for my story about the ringing phone and the mysterious orange flash. The police made a greater show of concern, and asked if I wouldn't mind coming to the station in the morning to file an accident report. I assured them I'd been planning to drop by anyway.

It had taken forty minutes to wade through the stack of accident-report forms. I was about halfway done when an earnest-looking young plainclothesman named MacLeavy tapped my shoulder, handed me the cold pack—one of those blue liquid ones—and told me Lieutenant Chasfield wanted to see me when I finished with the paperwork.

I'd been waiting in Chasfield's office for close to an hour. After counting holes, I nosed around a little. Photos on the green steel desk told me that he was married and had three daughters. Two citations for valor hung on the walls, along with a marksmanship certificate and a fair number of testimonials to the lieutenant's charity works.

There were photographs on the walls too. Most of them showed a beefy, red-nosed guy standing beside the mayor, a baseball player, or a department official. The red-nosed guy, who I assumed was Chasfield, had an expression of strained forbearance in each of the pictures, as though the photographer had interrupted him in the middle of a great story.

None of this helped to ease the throbbing in my head, so I went back to staring at the ceiling. Much of it was stained with brown wet patches. One of them bore a comforting resemblance to Ohio, where I'd lived for six years after my mother remarried. I hadn't been back since she died. I wondered if there was any steady work for magicians in Ohio.

"Paul Galliard?" said a voice.

I snapped my head forward, the cold pack fell to the floor. An older version of the figure in the photographs hovered in the doorway. I stood up. "I'm Galliard. Are you Lieutenant Chasfield?"

"Uh," he said, stepping forward to shake my hand. He sized me up pretty carefully as he lowered himself into the padded vinyl chair behind his desk. I had a good look at him too.

Chasfield appeared to be in his mid-sixties. He moved like a guy who wasn't used to carrying around thirty extra pounds, though he looked as if he'd had some time to get used to it. He had thinning brown hair and a strong, deeply lined forehead. His nose was not only red but also crooked, pitted, and hairy. Chasfield's blue eyes, by contrast, were those of an eager young boy waiting for the rabbit to pop out of the hat.

"Understand you've got a homicide to report, uh?" He shuffled some papers on his desk. "But no evidence."

"I had evidence, as I explained to the officers who came to my apartment, but it was destroyed. In my apartment."

Chasfield sucked in his cheeks and puffed them out

rapidly. "The responding officers' reports say you had yourself a gas explosion. Seems you left your stove on."

"No chance. There's no way I left the stove on. Besides, the fire wasn't even in the kitchen."

"Doesn't have to be."

"Look, Lieutenant, I know I've been asking your men to believe quite a bizarre story, but I had the evidence to prove it. The poison balloons. Doesn't it seem funny to you that those balloons were among the only things destroyed in that fire?"

Chasfield put on a pair of horn-rimmed bifocals that really showcased the nose. "Uh," he said. "The poison balloons. I heard all about it from MacLeavy. You story is developing a real following down in the locker room. Seems some of the boys are already telling it to their kids, you know, along with 'Goldilocks and the Three Bears'?"

"I have someone who can verify it. A lab technician."

Chasfield looked at me over his bifocals. "A police lab technician?"

"No."

"Then it won't hold up. Look, kid, I've been on the force a long time, and I've swallowed some pretty tall tales, but you've got to be reasonable. They say you want me to reopen the files on this guy, this—"

"Josef Schneider."

"Right. You expect me to reopen the case, possibly overturn a coroner's ruling, all without court evidence? Best I can do is look into it, go over the records, uh?" I noticed that he said "uh" quite a bit. "I don't promise anything."

I stared up at the ceiling, thinking about Ohio. "Why bother?" I asked. "I mean, you must get a fair number of crackpots through here. You obviously think I'm one of them. Why humor me?"

Chasfield's eyes swept the room for a moment, as though the answer might be hanging in one of his picture frames. "Maybe I feel I owe you something," he said.

"How's that?"

He took off his glasses and tossed them on the desk. "Kid, they don't just show anyone off the street in here to see me. When I heard you were in the station, I asked to see you special." He stared at me hard, looking for something in my face. The blue eyes no longer looked quite so young and eager. "Kid, you know who I am?"

"Lieutenant Harvey Chasfield, Senior Homicide Detective?"

"Kid, I'm the man who shot your father."

We sat looking at each other across the desk for a while. Suddenly it came to me where I'd heard the name before.

I wanted a drink when I left Chasfield's office, but 9:45 is a little early to start drinking if you expect to vanish rabbits and juggle Indian clubs later in the day. I decided to settle for a strong cup of coffee.

They'd just finished with the rush-hour crowd at Frieda's pastry shop when I stepped off the bus twenty minutes later. Empty mugs and abandoned newspapers littered the tables, but nobody seemed in a great hurry to clear them off. Three waitresses in khaki pants and blue shirts sat placidly at private corners of the shop, enjoying their own morning coffee and newspapers. The first of the day's soap operas was going on a television near the door, with an elderly gentleman advising a distraught young woman to take another shot at happiness.

Nobody looked up when I came in. The morning coffee break is something of an institution at Frieda's.

Frieda herself sat with a pot of tea at her usual table near the counter. "Paul!" she said, as I walked over. "So soon out of the hospital! Are you sure you should be up walking around? Sit, I'll bring you some tea." She started to rise but I waved her back down and went around the counter to pour a cup of coffee.

"You were not yourself when I visited in the hospital," she said when I sat down across from her. "They would not allow me in. Tests, they said. The cakes I left, did you get them?"

"I did. Thank you for bringing them. I used them to buy my freedom."

She studied my face. "You look very pale, very . . . chalklike. And there is something bothering you. Otherwise you do not come to see me."

"It was kind of a rough night. I didn't get much sleep."

"That is nothing new. You never sleep. Always the dark circles."

"I just wanted to see how you were doing, how you're holding up."

She didn't buy it. A wry smile broke across her face, the same smile I used to get when I volunteered to demonstrate my new "vanishing carrot cake" trick. She set down her teacup, closed her eyes and pressed her palms together, mimicking a mind-reading routine her brother had taught me at that very table. "O Great Swami," she intoned, putting an effective little vibrato in her voice, "peer into the mind of the troubled young man I see before me. What disturbs him so? Answer, answer."

"Cigarette lighter," I said.

"What?"

"Answer, answer. It was Josef's code for a cigarette lighter. Or a comic book, depending on what kind of crowd he was playing."

Frieda reached across the table and gave my hands a squeeze. "I know that you miss him," she said. "I do also. Very much."

I nodded. "Frieda, I didn't see too much of Josef in the last few weeks. Did you notice—please bear with me here—did you notice anything strange about him just before he died?"

The wry smile returned to her lips. "This is why you have come to see me? You are playing the detective now?

**70**

To be a magician is not exciting enough? Perhaps next you will want to be riding the elephant in the circus? Walking on the high wire?" She took a sip of tea. "Paul. Take a moment and try to think clearly. I know what Josef meant to you. Don't you think it may be—"

"Try to think clearly," I echoed. "I wonder how many times I've heard that over the last few days? It's enough to make a fellow insecure."

"I am only—"

"Frieda, humor me. I'm not asking if he was involved in any high-speed car chases, or if he had any midnight meetings under the clock at the Biltmore. I just want to know if anything out of the ordinary was going on in his life. Anything. Like a change in eating habits, or unexpected phone calls."

Frieda warmed her hands around her teacup. A look of resignation came over her face. Middle age had not dimmed her considerable beauty. She remained elegant in a decidedly European way, with a high forehead, strong chin, and sharp nose that somehow combined to give a very soft effect. The high lace collars she wore made her look pleasantly Victorian.

"Yes," she said, raising her cup again, "Josef acted strangely the last few days. But I know what the trouble was. He was nervous. Nervous and excited about that television program that all of you were going to do—"

"All of *them* were going to do, Frieda. I wasn't going to do it."

She gave me a beautifully indulgent smile. "He was going to talk to you. He was going to make you audition along with him. All of them from the old days—Clément, Nussbaum—they all wanted to audition. They wanted you to do it too."

One of the cable networks was putting together a two-hour special to celebrate the thirtieth anniversary of the premiere of *Magic Cavalcade*, the show where my father got his start. That was what Mindy Kramer, the perky assistant producer, had been calling about a couple of days earlier. The plan was to feature as many of the original cast as possible, alongside the best—or at least the most affordable—of today's magicians.

"Don't get me wrong, Frieda. Ordinarily I'd jump at that kind of exposure, but the producers only want me on one condition. They want me to re-create my father's act, right down to the trick he was doing when he died."

"Josef seemed to think he could persuade you to do it."

"Well, all right," I said, "suppose he passed a miracle and talked me into doing the show. You're sure that's it? He wasn't the type to get all worked up about a magic show. Even one on television. Are you sure that's the only unusual thing you noticed?"

"I am sorry, Mr. Hawkshaw, that is all I noticed. What more were you expecting?"

I got up from the table and went around the counter to pour myself another cup of coffee. What more had I been expecting? It was a good question. Maybe I'd hoped for some kind of message. *By the way, my good sister, if I should happen to be poisoned any time in the very near future, please tell young Paul . . .* what? I set the coffee carafe down on the burner and returned to the table. Earlier I'd decided not to tell her about the balloons until I absolutely had to. I think I honestly believed that Schneider would have wanted it that way. I probably should have told her everything right then. Maybe things would have come out differently.

Instead, always a sucker for the pithy remark, I said, "Boy, this is good coffee."

"You are not listening to me, Paul."

I looked across the table. Frieda's eyes were wet, her expression fixed on something far away.

"You don't understand," she said. "Every time Josef came home from one of those magic shows he had to lie down for the rest of the day. It was too much for him. I told him again and again. I said, 'Josef, no more magic shows for the children. They wear you out. Your face gets red.' I said that to him."

"I know you did," I said.

"I told him, 'You come and work in the shop. You give up the hocus-pocus.' Did he listen?"

"Of course not."

"Then, after the first attack, I said—"

"What first attack? A heart attack?"

"Seven months ago."

"Frieda, why didn't anyone tell me that? Where was I?"

"What would you have done?"

"For Christ's sake, Frieda! I'd have done something! I'd have—I don't know—talked to him at least. Helped him out, visited more . . ."

Frieda took a sip of her tea. "You know what he was like. He didn't want for people to know. And even then he wouldn't slow down. He kept working and working, thinking that somehow it would—that it would be like the old days. When he was famous. Then this television show came along, and he worked even harder. That is what killed him, Paul."

A woman with three children came into the shop, collared one of Frieda's clerks and made a lot of noise about ordering a birthday cake. That ended the morning coffee break. I remembered that I had a show to do later that afternoon; a birthday party in Jersey City.

"Frieda," I said, "I didn't mean to upset you. I'm probably making too much of this. I just can't help feeling that I should have—"

She reached across the table and poured a packet of sugar into my coffee. "Drink," she said. "It's good for you. You look as if you could use the energy."

We sat for a bit longer while she questioned me closely about my episode in the hospital. Then I went on to tell her about the fire in my apartment, giving her the official version of what had happened. Her eyes seemed to brighten when I told her I'd have to move out of my building.

"That reminds me," she said, "there is something I have wanted to talk to you about. It is about Josef's things. I will need some help moving them out of the room upstairs."

"Sure," I said. "Whenever."

"Could you come up there with me now for a moment? Just to see what needs to be done?" I followed her back through the kitchen to the black-painted steel steps that led up to Schneider's apartment.

Over the years I have lost much of my enthusiasm for magic. A trip to the magic store is no longer an occasion of wonder. The magicians I once revered as gods now seem distressingly mortal. I have become, to use a word of no little significance to magicians, disillusioned in all but one particular. Schneider's apartment above the pastry shop had lost none of its hold over me. The room, with its dusty relics and casually displayed memorabilia, never failed to set my heart pounding, just as it did when I was eleven years old. If anything, given my hard-won knowledge of New York City real estate, the place seemed even more remarkable with the passage of time.

"What am I going to do with this place?" Frieda wondered aloud. "I could rent it out as storage—no doubt I would make a fortune—but that would mean clearing out Josef's things. I am not ready to do that, not yet. But who would want it as it is?"

She stepped into the room, running her hand along the edge of the Floating Lady equipment. "A further worry. Whoever took over this place would have direct access to the pastry shop, night and day. I could not ask them to crawl up and down the fire escape. No. They would have to use the stairs, and come through the kitchen. It would have to be someone I could trust with the keys to my shop. Where would I find such a person?"

"Frieda," I began, "I—"

"Where would I find such a person?" she repeated. "That is quite a puzzler, as I have so often heard you say."

I stood more or less dumbstruck while she made a slow circuit of the room, lingering every so often over a photograph or piece of apparatus.

"I think I had best get back down to the shop," she said after a while. "You stay here for a moment." She walked to the stairs. "If you think of a suitable tenant, please be sure to tell me."

I listened to her footfalls on the stairs, then I sat down at the small dressing table and looked at myself in the bulb-lined mirror. My cheeks were flushed and there was a goofy grin on my face that I couldn't seem to control.

A small pewter frame sat on the dressing table amid tubes of dried makeup. It held a picture of Schneider that I'd never seen before. I reached for it but couldn't grab hold; my hand passed right through the picture and frame as though they were made of some kind of spirit ectoplasm. I could only laugh. Even in death the old man still had a couple of tricks up his sleeve. Years ago he'd loved toying around with "ghostly image" mirror boxes. Employing an optical principle I didn't entirely understand, he'd managed to arrange a concave mirror, a hidden light bulb, and a reflective tray so as to create endlessly surprising little holograms. He cut a hole in the top of the dressing table so that anything he placed in the upper drawer would appear to be sitting on the surface, a few inches in front of the mirror. "Look, Paul," he'd say. "There is a dollar for the stalwart young man who carries my magical case! Go on, take it!" I'd reach, but the image of the dollar would melt around my fingers, as though I'd passed my hand in front of a movie projector. I fell for it every time.

Idly, I swept my hand through Schneider's image a few more times. Then I pulled open the drawer, slid a mirror aside, and lifted out the actual picture frame.

The photograph showed Schneider as a very young man, in Austria, before the decline in his fortunes that accompanied the hasty emigration to America. He stood with his feet wide apart on some grassy hillock, hands clasped behind his back, an expression of quiet resolve on his face. Though he would later prove to be the salvation of my childhood, seeing him as he appeared in that photograph—confident and hopeful—made me wish that he'd found some more respectable line of work.

After a few minutes I pulled the drawer open to replace the picture. Something behind the image box caught my eye. I reached in and withdrew a bulky envelope with a slit along the flap. Inside was a small bundle tied with a red silken cord. I knew immediately what it was, but still I rolled it over in my hands a couple of times as if it might turn out to be something else entirely. Then I set the bundle cautiously on the table, perhaps hoping that like the picture frame, it would fade and disappear.

I was starting to wish that I'd found a more respectable line of work too.

# Chapter 7

Clara stood in the doorway of her kitchen, arms folded, watching as I fussed with my ingredients.

"I don't know which is worse, Paul," she said. "Waiting for you to spill the beans about what's been going on these last two days, or waiting for you to cook the damn hamburgers."

"Don't rush me, newswoman," I said, poking at a pile of raw meat with my finger. "Don't rush me on either score. A good magician knows when to hold back. It's all part of the buildup. The buildup to the big reveal."

"The reveal of what? This deep, dark secret you've been keeping, or dinner? I've been waiting two days for the hamburgers. Any more buildup tonight and I'll send out for Chinese."

"I'm sorry about that. I really am. That's what the flowers were for. I was hoping to soften you up."

"Nice touch. I'm softened. I'm positively limp. Now, come on. Talk."

I bent low over the chopping board, dicing some onions with exaggerated care. "Are you sure Franklin isn't going to want a hamburger?" I asked.

"He went to bed over an hour ago. I generally give him dinner before he goes to sleep. Stop stalling."

I searched for and located a large ceramic mixing bowl. "Got any Worcestershire sauce?" I asked.

"Maybe you'll talk if I ply you with alcohol," Clara said, sliding past me to get a couple of beers from the refrigerator. I could tell she wasn't really all that aggravated or impatient with me. I could tell by the way she rested her hand on my back as she moved about the narrow kitchen. Call it an intuitive gift.

Clara looked great in casual clothes, I noticed. She had come to the door wearing a man's white shirt, jeans, and thick wool socks. The jeans were just plain blue denims—moderately faded, no showy rips or patches. Also, there was no designer label on the back pocket. I learned this through close study. The shirt had somebody else's monogram on the pocket, maybe her ex-husband's. I'd never heard her mention his name. Whenever she mentioned him, which was seldom, she referred to him as "Mr. Sensitivity." He'd walked out three years earlier, but not without leaving some parting gifts. You could still see one of the scars over her right eye, and another one along her left ear when she wore her hair back.

"You're not playing fair, you know," she said. "You've stood me up two nights running. I won't say your excuses aren't good. They're fantastic, actually. I mean, we make plans for a quiet dinner at home, and you wind up in the hospital. Fine. Don't take it personally, I tell myself. Reschedule. Then what happens? Your apartment blows up. I tell you, Galliard, it's enough to rattle a woman's confidence." She twisted open the beer bottles and handed me one. "What some men won't do to get out of cooking a meal."

I dumped the meat and oinions into a bowl and splashed in some Worcestershire sauce. "Where do you keep the cayenne?" I asked. I'm an indifferent cook, but I've found that people tend to credit you with enormous skill if you affect a preference for one kind of pepper over another.

She handed me a spice shaker and continued to favor me with her views on unreliable men while I shaped the meat into patties and sautéed them, briskly. In a few minutes we were seated on the floor of her living room, eating off trays in front of the fireplace. I thought it all rather cozy and romantic. Clara had a different agenda.

"You mentioned finding something in a drawer? Something important?"

"Some hamburger, eh?" I said.

"The hamburgers are divine."

"Juicy and flavorful, right?"

"I never knew it could be like this. You've redefined the form. Now please, tell me what's going on."

With a shrug, I handed over the bundle I'd taken from the drawer of Schneider's dressing table. I went back to eating while she looked at it.

"I've been in a daze all afternoon," I told her. "I gave a show out in Jersey City, I don't even remember getting there. What I *do* remember is substituting origami figures for balloon animals—"

"Paul, this looks like an old magic wand."

"It is."

"So?"

"Notice anything unusual about it?"

"It's broken."

"And?"

"The pieces are tied with a silk ribbon."

"Right."

"I repeat: So?"

I got up and went into the kitchen for two more bottles of beer. She had set the broken wand on the floor near the fireplace when I got back. "Perhaps you're not up on your magic lore," I said, lowering myself back down beside her. "When a magician dies, he's given what's called a 'broken wand' service. His peers from the magic society recite something about the bonds of the conjuring fraternity, then they break a magic wand over the coffin."

"Okay, so this is the wand they broke for Schneider," Clara said, picking up her hamburger. "What's so incredible about that?"

"If it is, it came through some rather remarkable channels to get here. To the best of my knowledge, the wand broken at Schneider's funeral is still lying on top of his coffin under six feet of dirt. I was the one who threw it there. Besides, that wand was the cheapo kind—balsa wood. This one's different. Take a good look."

She didn't. She had the look of someone who suddenly realizes that the person next to her in the stalled elevator is a carnival geek.

"Just hear me out," I said. "If you still think I'm deluded, I'll leave. Quietly. I'll even get help. You might be able to do a feature: 'Crazed Magician Deludes Self, Others.' "

"How about, 'Promising Scholar Fails to Escape Specter of Father'?"

"Funny you should mention him. Take a look at that wand. It's not the sort of thing you'd find in a Mysto magic set. It's not your typical wand at all."

"And why is that, pray?"

"Come on, Clara. Meet me halfway on this. Look at it. It's an expensive piece of work—ebony wood, silver tips. Custom made. It's like something you'd have seen in the hands of one of the Herrmanns, or John Maskelyne, even. But that particular wand belonged to a very special magician of my acquaintance."

"Not Schneider?"

"Not Schneider."

Something fell into place for her. She set down her hamburger and pushed some hair back from her face as she looked over at me. Her sad gray eyes seemed a shade sadder. "Your father?"

"Exactly. Galliard *père*. Of sainted memory and spectacular exit. That's one of his wands, I'm positive."

Clara chose her words carefully. "Can you really be so sure? I mean, isn't it possible that—"

I cut her off. "Look," I said, putting my plate down on the tray, "I know whereof I speak. That wand is as distinctive as a fingerprint. It's a relic. A relic from the days when magic meant real theater, when magicians lavished money on every detail of their shows. They used the best of everything in those days—the finest silks, real gold fittings on their apparatus, the works."

"Production value," Clara said.

"It was something more than that. All modern magic—by that I mean from the Palais Royal forward—"

"But of course."

"Look, Miss Bidwell, you wanted an explanation."

"I did, I know. Go on."

"It's really very simple," I said. "The plain fact is, magic ain't what it used to be. Not even close. All modern magic—even that of a hundred years ago—it labors under the weight of an earlier and far more glorious era when magicians were something more than stage performers. In the good old days—the era of Cheops, for example, or the Arthurian age—magicians were the confidants of kings. Sometimes they were even revered as gods. As late as the mid-nineteenth century—1855, I think it was, or 'fifty-six—Robert-Houdin was called upon by the French government to put down a peasant uprising in Algeria. This actually happened. He produced cannonballs from an empty hat, robbed a muscular soldier of his strength, that sort of thing. All to convince the rebel leaders of France's power. Nowadays you'd send a helicopter gunship; in those days you sent a well-equipped magician."

I took a swallow of beer. "The whole point is that there was a time when the art of conjuring was something more than light entertainment—more than Mr. Wonder and his scantily clad assistant toughing it out at the Elks Club, more than the fat guy selling tricks and novelties from a stool down at the mall. The charm and the power of contemporary magic, I've always thought, is that echo, however faint, of the grand tradition." I took another sip of beer, a little surprised and embarrassed by my own effusion. Clara didn't seem to mind.

"Professor," she said, "you know how I love it when you get all misty-eyed about the past. I could listen to you all night. But what's any of that got to do with finding a broken old wand in a dead man's desk?"

"I was only trying to establish a *context*, as we used to say in the History Department. I was hoping to make all this a little more credible. People today just don't understand that the study and performance of magic carries a —a *symbology*, if you will—that every magician, from the ten-year-olds to the pros, understands or senses to one extent or another. That's why a broken wand is a very different thing to me than it is to you."

"What are we talking about here? Superstition?"

"Necessity. Watch this." I got up and tapped a cigarette out of a pack on the mantelpiece. "Observe. I take the cigarette, snap off the filter, and tear the paper up the side. Now I've got a handful of loose tobacco, a filter, and a little wad of cigarette paper. See?" I held out my palm for inspection.

"Intriguing," Clara said.

"Now I ball up my fingers and—say! Look here! A magic wand! Just what I need!" I picked up the pieces of the broken wand from the coffee table and waved them over my closed fist. "And now, I uncurl my fingers and—can it be? Yes! The cigarette is fully restored!"

I could see that Clara was impressed, very much in spite of herself. It's good, strong, close-up. Only Slydini does that one better than I do.

"Now then," I said, sitting down on the floor again, "I know that you like to think of me as a god among men, but the truth is, I don't really have any magic powers."

Clara brought her hands to her cheeks, miming astonishment.

"It's true. I used a clever sleight of hand to bring that off. And though I hate to admit it, the wand covered that sleight so you wouldn't see it. Schneider used to call it 'unseen magic.' It's a little crutch we all use. And because wands are partly a crutch themselves, many magicians try to make theirs as distinctive and flashy as possible. My father was one such magician. He had five wands, in fact. Each of them was a slightly different size and weight, for use in each of the five different phases of his act. He even had a special carrying case for them. He took these things very seriously. So it kind of sets one to thinking when his friend Josef Schneider drops dead under—hear me out on this—under mysterious circumstances, having received one of my lamented father's custom-made wands—snapped in half, mind you—only days before." I set down the restored cigarette and the broken wand. "That concludes this portion of tonight's lecture." I picked up my half-eaten hamburger. "I believe the young woman in the white shirt had a question?"

Clara fingered the red silk ribbon tied around the pieces of the wand. "Paul, don't get mad at me, but isn't it just possible—and more likely—that your father gave the wand to Schneider years ago, that Schneider broke it somehow by accident and decided to keep the pieces around as a memento?"

"What about the envelope? It had a fairly recent postmark on it."

"That doesn't mean much. I'm always putting things into envelopes, it's as convenient a place as any to put something. Even a used envelope."

"Do you know anything about how my father died?"

"Not really. All I know is it involved a gunshot accident, and it was ruled 'death by misadventure.' "

"Are you serious?"

"Well, yes. I do my homework. I was looking for something in the newspaper morgue the other day. I pulled his obit."

"It was slightly more complicated than that." I set down my empty beer bottle. "Look, if we're going to get into this, we'll need some harder liquor."

"I have some Scotch."

"That'll do."

Clara went into the kitchen and brought back two glasses filled with ice. The bottle came from a little oak cabinet in the corner. She poured while I talked.

"Do you remember a TV show called *Magic Cavalcade*? In the late fifties? It was a magic revue, broadcast live on Sunday nights from the Olympia Theater. My father was a regular. Schneider was a frequent guest."

"Isn't that the one you were telling me about?" Clara asked. "The one they're planning to re-create? I don't think I ever actually watched it when it was on originally."

I nodded, taking a sip of the Scotch she handed me. "I'm not surprised, bunch of men in silly evening clothes, wasting their potential, avoiding graduate school. Not your cup of tea, really. Anyway, one night in 1959, my father introduced a new effect on the show. He called it 'The Death-Defying Bullet Catch.' "

"Bullet catch?" Clara asked. "Your father caught bullets? Stepped in front of loaded guns?"

I nodded again. "Magicians have been catching bullets almost since the invention of gunpowder. Here's where our earlier lesson comes into play. You're aware that many actors are superstitious about performing *Macbeth*? That's nothing compared with the curse that supposedly hangs over the bullet-catch effect."

Clara broke in. "I notice you used the word 'superstitious' there. . . ."

"Most superstitions evolve from fact. Productions of *Macbeth* have been plagued by accidents from Shakespeare's time on. It's the same thing with the bullet catch. At least twelve magicians have died performing it, possibly more. The most famous would have to be Chung Ling Soo."

"Let me guess . . . a Chinese gentleman?"

"Not exactly, but he did a very Chinese act—exotic costumes, flaming dragons, all the classic Chinese effects. It must have been something to see. The bullet catch was his trademark. It was supposed to be a dramatization of how Chung Ling Soo survived the Boxer Rebellion. He did it hundreds of times without a hitch, always the same way, always with the same pair of old-fashioned twelve-bore muzzle-loading rifles. Two assistants pointed the rifles at a small china plate that he held in front of his chest. As the riflemen fired, Chung would sweep his hand through the air, supposedly plucking the bullets in mid-flight. Well, one night the trick went wrong. The guns went off and Chung caught a round in the chest. They say he was greatly surprised. He had the presence of mind to have his assistants ring down the curtain, then he died."

I took a sip of my drink. A gulp, actually. "As you might imagine, nobody went near the bullet catch for a while. Houdini made some noise about doing it a few years later, but Kellar talked him out of it. 'We can't afford to lose Houdini,' he said." I could feel a tightness forming at the base of my skull. I hadn't actually talked about this with anyone in over five years.

Clara reached for the cigarette I had restored and struck a match. I watched as though it were the most captivating thing I'd ever seen. "Well," I resumed, my voice sounding reedy, "in 1959 my father's career was on the wane and he was casting about for a big effect. Naturally he thought of the bullet catch. The truth is, it's not that difficult to do. It's well known that Chung Ling Soo died through neglect of his equipment. His rifles had a false chamber to prevent the gunpowder from igniting the live round. A crack formed in one of the rifles, so that every time the gun was used, a few grains of gunpowder trickled down near the flash hole of the live chamber. Finally the accumulated charge went off.

"My father felt sure he could avoid making the same mistake. I'm told he was quite confident. He used one of the best-made guns available, a .557 Nitro Express, and worked out what he considered to be a foolproof method. He even added a few touches like a sheet of glass suspended at mid-stage. The audience would actually see the glass shatter when the gun went off. Also, he'd use only one rifleman, who would be a police officer, not a hired assistant. In fact, it would be the police academy's star marksman, whose name that year was Officer Harvey Chasfield."

Clara shifted her body toward me, the very picture of attention. I didn't look directly at her. Mostly I kept my eyes on the fire. Now and then my eyes drifted a few degrees to the right, where I'd see my own reflection on the darkened screen of the television.

"I can still remember the buildup. Seeing my dad's picture in the paper, hearing the announcements on the radio. 'The crowning effect of Galliard's career; he takes his rightful place among the masters of all time.' That kind of thing. So the big night comes, and—" My voice cracked, just a little. "Dry throat," I said. My glass was empty, so I picked up Clara's. "Aren't you going to drink this? Don't you know there are children in India who go to bed sober each night?"

"You don't have to go on with this if you don't want. I think I can guess what happened next."

"Your guess is as good as mine. I didn't actually see it—" I gave a hoarse little laugh. "It was past my bedtime."

Clara stayed silent for a decent interval while I looked at some intriguing hot embers in the fireplace.

"Tell me one thing," she said after a while. "After all of that, why the hell did you become a magician?"

I laughed. "Still trying to get me back into a more respectable line of work?"

"It's a perfectly good question. I mean, let's face it—"

"Believe me, as a kid I never considered magic as a career. Quite the opposite. Even after Schneider came along, even after I started to get good, I just couldn't see following in my father's ill-fated footsteps. But in a way, I couldn't avoid it. All my life I've been a museum piece. People hear my name and they say, 'Galliard? Isn't that the guy who—' Then they get this terribly embarrassed look on their faces."

"Come on, Paul. Plenty of people have overcome their parents' . . . um, notoriety."

"It's more than that. In spite of what happened to my father, I still found myself drawn to magic. It's hard to explain. From the day Schneider taught me my first trick, I found I had an almost absurd facility for magic. I've never had to practice as hard as other magicians. It's as if—"

"As if you were born to it? As if fate had guided you? I don't believe it for a minute."

"I'm not asking you to."

"That doesn't answer my question. Why did you go into it?"

"Well, it has to do with a lost library book."

"Come on. I asked a serious question."

"And I gave you a serious answer."

"You left graduate school and became a professional magician because of a lost library book?"

I set down my glass, reflecting that Scotch and attractive women could make me say almost anything. "It was my second year of grad school, second-semester registration. I'd been in this huge gymnasium all day, standing in lines. Lines to preregister, lines to pull computer punch cards, lines to pay this or that fee, lines to get my student I.D. Finally I'm standing in the line to pay the tuition bill, and I find out there's a little pink slip, a stop on my registration because of a lost library book. Cheever's *The Brigadier and the Golf Widow*. The same thing had happened the semester before, and I'd spent three weeks trying to get it straightened out. Finally, I'd paid to replace the book they said I'd lost, only to have it turn up in the stacks the next day. I spent three more weeks trying to get my money back. By that time it had become a point of honor. This second time, though, I just snapped. I'd been standing in line all day, waiting to write a check with far too many zeros on it, only to find out I would be denied the privilege because of some book that the library had lost in my name."

"Calm down. You're going to wake up Franklin."

"Sorry. It still infuriates me. Anyway, I walked out. I withdrew from school the next day. Didn't even have to stand in line. Not a long line, anyway. Had my first professional booking by the end of the week."

"I don't buy it. Nothing's that pat. It sounds as if you really planned to become a magician all the time, like graduate school was some kind of denial. Maybe you're confronting—"

"Spare me."

"Fine. So now you're a magician. What's next? Are you planning to go the whole way? Maybe catch a few bullets yourself one fine day?"

"Not likely."

"Isn't that the whole point of this? The *Magic Cavalcade* reunion they've been calling you about? Don't they have it in mind for you to re-create your father's act? I assume that means the bullet trick."

"Even if I wanted to, I couldn't possibly do the bullet catch."

"Why's that?"

"I don't know what went wrong. I don't even know how it was supposed to be done. I know more about Chung Ling Soo's death than my own father's. A few years back I tried to figure it out. I asked Schneider about it and he said, 'Sometimes it is best not to question the workings of fate.' That was helpful, let me tell you. The newspaper accounts weren't much better. They raised more questions than they answered. Like the thing about Ho-Ho. The papers were full of that at the time."

"What?"

"My father's right-hand man. His name was Horst Katzenbacher, but I only know that from the newspapers.

I remember him as Ho-Ho. He used to give me horsey rides. The stories all say that he dropped out of sight for a couple of hours on the night in question, and when he turned up again, he had a broken nose and a black eye. Wouldn't say a word about what happened. Or about the wands."

"The wands?"

"The night my father died, every last one of his wands disappeared. They say his assistants looked high and low. Some imaginative types speculated that my father took them with him to the grave. The point is, nobody ever saw them again after that night."

"Until now."

I looked at the broken wand next to the fireplace. "Until now," I repeated.

# Chapter 8

The coffee at Smithson's Grill always has a shiny soap slick floating at the top. Maybe it's their way of reassuring you that they really do wash the mugs between uses. It's the kind of place where you need some reassurance.

I was the only guy in there that noon wearing a top hat and tails. It drew a few raised eyebrows at the lunch counter, but I didn't care. I had a higher purpose. I was there for the Manhattan/Bronx Thursday Magic & Lunch Club.

The Thursday Magic & Lunch Club got its start on May 12, 1904. It's possible to be precise about the date because it was an anniversary of sorts; on that day fifteen years earlier, Washington Irving Bishop passed away for the third and final time.

Bishop, who had billed himself as the "First and World-Eminent Mind-Reader," may have also been the first magician to understand the heady power of self-promotion. Early in his career he had discovered that he could generate a huge amount of free publicity by covering his eyes with a thick blindfold and guiding a team of horses through Manhattan at a full gallop. A cataleptic, Bishop often collapsed in an apparently lifeless heap at the climax of his own performance. In the throes of one of these seizures, his heartbeat and breathing would become almost imperceptible. Twice he'd actually been pronounced dead, only to recover—blinking and rubbing his eyes—a few hours later.

One night Bishop suffered an attack during a particularly draining demonstration at a New York actors' club. Doctors were summoned, and unaware of Bishop's catalepsy, they administered some of the common remedies of the day—electric shock and injections of brandy. Such treatments, however, were specifically prohibited by a warning letter Bishop usually carried in his pocket. For some reason he'd neglected to take it with him that night. One hopes, therefore, that the shock and brandy injections killed the magician early on. If not, the autopsy that was performed later that evening surely did. One version of the story, advanced by Bishop's mother, has it that jealous physicians performed the autopsy prematurely, in order to make off with the mind reader's brain.

Though Bishop had shunned the company of magicians in life, his death created a legend in the magic fraternity. Within ten years Bishop's status soared from that of minor performer to magic martyr. While Bishop lived, the famous illusionist Howard Thurston would have crossed the street to avoid meeting him. After the premature autopsy, however, Thurston did much to keep the mind reader's memory alive. In 1904, seeking to observe the fifteenth anniversary of Bishop's death in proper solemnity, Thurston invited his mentor Harry Kellar to share in a quiet toast at the Morehouse, a restaurant on lower Broadway.

The Morehouse in those days was much prized by vaudeville artists for the restful atmosphere it afforded prior to performance. Magicians were secretly glad of the high prices—they kept out the class of people who'd be likely to attend magic shows. Kellar found this particularly useful, since he liked to tell people that he spent the hours before curtain time in solitary meditation.

Thurston was a regular at the restaurant. So was Theo Hardeen, who was seated with his brother Harry Houdini at an adjacent table when Thurston and Kellar sat down to their Bishop memorial lunch. Thrown together by chance, the four greatest magicians of the era formed a sort of round table, one-upping each other's card tricks and getting uproariously drunk—all except for Houdini, who was a teetotaler.

When the time came to withdraw into their respective theaters, Thurston wrestled the check away from Houdini, who, true to form, insisted rather stridently on repaying the debt the following week. Within a month the meetings had become a regular event. The name of Washington Irving Bishop was rarely mentioned.

Touring schedules being what they were, the four original members seldom appeared after the first few Thursdays, but other notable magicians came and went through the years. During the Depression, the round table moved to the more modest Plumtree Room on Eighth Avenue, where it remained for nearly four decades, until some sort of embarrassing accident occurred involving doves, fire, and chintz curtains.

The new quarters at Smithson's, in the lobby of the once-grand Ruggles Hotel, afforded the club's later incarnations exactly what they were after: a quiet table, decent pastrami, and indulgent waitresses who were always willing to pick a card, any card. Also, flame-resistant curtains.

The round table's current members had little in common with their august founders. They were old men whose moments in the spotlight, if they had come at all, had been brief and quickly forgotten. When I was a child, however, they had seemed to me to be great men.

Edouard Clément came in first, pointing the way

with his silver-knobbed walking stick. He was small and wiry, with white hair slicked down under a feathered fedora and green eyes that seemed to take in everything and find it all faintly amusing. He'd been a great card mechanic until arthritis got him. Now his hands were constricted in flesh-colored canvas braces that looked like fingerless gloves.

Jacob Nussbaum followed at Clément's elbow, towering over the smaller man like a docile black bear. He wore a two-tone "loafer" jacket, a white shirt, green tie, and brown houndstooth slacks. On a younger man the outfit might have been considered witty. Nussbaum's act, like his clothes, hadn't varied in more than thirty years. The centerpiece was a nine-minute dove routine, climaxed with a vanishing bird cage and a joke about flying south for the winter. Somehow I'd never tired of it. Age had been kinder to Nussbaum than to Clément, and since his act had never required any great skill, he could still do it as well as ever.

With Schneider gone, the two of them were all that remained of Howard Thurston's round table. I watched them from across the room for a few minutes. Then I paid for my soapy coffee, felt in my pocket for the broken wand, and approached the table.

Clément spotted me first. "Well, well!" he said, half rising to greet me. "Young Galliard! Such a pleasure! You needn't have dressed for the occasion, though. We haven't required formal attire in some time."

"I had a show this morning," I said, pulling out a chair. "Not a real show, actually. I was demonstrating magic sets at Bloomingdale's. I didn't have time to change."

Clément laid his hands on the table. The joints looked dark and swollen. "So," he said. "Here you are. To what does our humble gathering owe this most gracious of honors?"

"I was in the neighborhood, thought I'd drop by for some help on my back palming."

"Need help with the old back palm?" asked Nussbaum eagerly. "Why, let's just see here . . ." He fumbled in his back pocket for a deck of cards.

"Jacob," Clément said gently, "Paul is just being kind. Twenty years ago he needed help with his back palm. Today he is a big shot. A television star. His back palm is good enough."

"Oh, I see." Nussbaum looked a little wounded.

"Actually," I said, "I came by to see how you were getting along. Catch up on the gossip."

"Have you heard about the *Magic Cavalcade* reunion?" Nussbaum asked. "I got a audition later this afternoon. I'm gonna show 'em my dove act."

"Me they didn't ask," Clément said. It was obviously a sore point. "Two seasons I did on that show, but did they ask? Did they ask the man who introduced 'The Dancing Waters of Troy' on their program?" He looked down at his arthritic braces. "I'm the first to admit that my sleights are not what they were, but I dare say I could bring off a stage illusion or two."

Nussbaum squirmed a bit at his own good fortune. "Maybe it was just a oversight that you didn't get asked. Maybe if you came with me this afternoon . . ."

"Perhaps." Clément rolled his eyes in my direction. "Young Mr. Galliard, here," he said. "*Him* they want."

"Hold it," I said. "They asked me for one reason and one reason only. They want me to re-create—"

"We know, we know," Nussbaum said. "You gonna do it?"

"What do you think?"

"Don't be so quick to refuse," Clément said. "You'll have the best magicians working today on that program. Sanderson, for instance. It won't be like the old days, but it'll be pretty good. They're even having that Chinese one they make such a fuss over . . . what's his name?"

"Yen Soo Kim," said Nussbaum.

"That's right. He'll be there. A good magician. Can you afford not to appear? It's the best exposure you'll ever have. Let's face the truth, Paul, these television commercials they're—they're—"

"They're not exactly going to secure my place in history," I said. "I know."

Clément nodded in agreement. "Paul, we've watched you grow into a fine young man. You have some bad habits, but you're a good magician. You have the touch. Even as a small boy you had the touch. You don't need advice from me anymore, but maybe you'll listen this one last time. Are you listening?" he asked.

I nodded.

"Do the bullet catch. You want to end up here in fifty years? I'm not so out of touch as I seem. I know what it takes to succeed these days. You do this special, maybe make a little splash in the papers. Next you do a Carson. Handsome young fellow like you, you'll do well. If he asks you back, you get a cable special, go on tour, sign some national endorsements. Gravy." He tapped my arm to drive the point home. "Gravy."

"I don't know," Nussbaum began. "That bullet catch . . ."

"That bullet catch nothing," Clément said heatedly. "What happened to your father was a fluke."

Nussbaum opened his mouth to say something, but thought better of it. A waiter came to take our lunch order, but Clément told him he needed more time to study the menu.

"I mean no disrespect, Paul," Clément continued when the waiter had gone. "You know that. But you shouldn't let what happened all those years ago hold you back. You're good. You *can* do the bullet catch. You *should* do it."

"But I won't," I said, keeping my tone deliberately casual, as if declining a refill on coffee. "I wouldn't even consider it without knowing what happened that night." I picked up a butter knife and did a baton twirl across my fingers. "Maybe if someone who was there could fill me in . . ."

A scared-rabbit look came into Clément's eyes. I'd seen the same look on Schneider's face a few times, whenever I asked him about my father's death. I'd always assumed he was simply reluctant to discuss such a painful subject with sensitive young Paul. I could see now there was something very different behind it.

"I told you before," Clément said. "A fluke. Your father was a fine magician, but sometimes—"

I completed his sentence for him. "But sometimes it's best not to question the workings of fate. I've been hearing that all my life, and I'm getting tired of it. You were there. You know what happened. Why has no one ever told me?"

Nussbaum leaned forward. "We thought it was gonna upset you to talk about it."

I did a snap vanish with the butter knife. "You two are quite a pair," I said. "First I sit here and listen to you advise me to go ahead with the bullet catch. Then in practically the same breath you say it's not important that I know what happened to my father when he did it. You expect me to step in front of the same rifle on live TV without knowing exactly what happened? 'Death by misadventure,' my ass."

"Paul—"

"Look, Edouard, I'm not the wide-eyed kid anymore. I know there's something going on. Some skeleton in the closet you've been hiding all these years. A few times I came close to getting it out of Josef—"

The two of them gave a start at the mention of Schneider's name. Nussbaum actually gasped.

I twirled the knife a few more times, then set it down and picked up a cloth napkin.

"Funny thing about Schneider, isn't it?" I said.

"What's funny about it?" Nussbaum said nervously.

"About Schneider. About his death." I spread the napkin flat on the table in front of me with slow, deliberate movements.

"Such a tragedy," Nussbaum declared. "He was my closest friend. We came over from Austria together, we—"

"About his murder."

Nussbaum and Clément exchanged looks. "Paul," Clément said, "you're being ridiculous. Like the time you—"

"Looked like a heart attack," I said, placing my butter knife in the center of the napkin. "Perfectly reasonable way for an old man with a heart condition to die. After all, he was exerting himself at the time. But we know better, don't we?"

I folded each corner of the napkin toward the center so that they covered the knife. Nussbaum pulled at his green tie.

"A single drop of poison in the nozzle of each balloon," I continued. "Isoproterenol. In a special penetrant solution, just to make it quicker. A few drops of glue to plug up his air pump, and Schneider's history."

I fixed my eyes on the folded napkin.

"Seems to me like a pretty elaborate way to kill a guy," I said. "Seems almost arcane. Unless . . ." I paused, my hand hovering over the napkin, as if the idea had just come to me. "Unless you're the kind of murderer who wants to throw a good scare into the victim's friends. Maybe you want to keep them quiet, or maybe you want something from them, I don't know. But it's definitely a murder with a message, the kind of murder that's understood by only a select few. Magicians only, and not all that many of them. And just so your intentions are fully understood, maybe you send around a few death threats."

"Paul, you're being ridiculous—"

I pinched a fold of the napkin between two fingers and flicked it open with a sharp, whip-crack motion of my wrist. It wasn't the butter knife that clattered onto the table. It was the broken wand. I let it lay there on the table until I was good and sure I'd made my point.

"Who else got one of these?" I asked.

Clément took out a handkerchief and gave his forehead a wipe.

"Both of us," he said.

# Chapter 9

The two elderly magicians kept quiet during the cab ride to Nussbaum's apartment. There, Clément and I sat in the kitchen while Nussbaum readied himself for his audition later that afternoon. Clément worked on a crossword puzzle from the morning paper. Despite the braces on his hands, he had no trouble holding a pencil, buttoning his shirt, or doing most of the hundreds of other daily tasks that require the use of one's fingers. One of the few things he couldn't do was hold a pack of cards. Not without dropping them. He still liked to watch other people work the deck, though.

"How long have you two had the wands?" I asked, reaching in my pocket for my red Aviators.

"Oh, a few weeks." I might as well have been asking when the irises had bloomed.

"They came through the mail?"

"Uh-huh."

"Broken?"

"Yes."

I set the cards on the kitchen table and ran through

some false cuts. "Doesn't that concern you a little bit?" I asked.

He bent low over the newspaper. "Just a little," he said.

"And you agree that the wands appear to be the ones missing from my father's collection?"

"So it would appear."

"Don't you find that a bit curious?"

"I wish you would come along to Jacob's audition this afternoon," he said, abruptly changing the subject. "It would mean a great deal to him."

"I really can't."

"He's been terribly nervous all week."

"I have to get out of these clothes and get my stuff moved over to Frieda's by noon tomorrow. My landlord wants me out of my old place by then."

He resumed work on the puzzle. "That's a pity," he said.

"The wands, Edouard. We were talking about the wands. Or rather, I was talking and you were hedging."

Clément gave a sigh of resignation and set down his mechanical pencil. "Paul, do you remember when you were about thirteen and thought the world revolved around that four-ace trick I did? The Elmsley Count routine, where the aces vanish from the deck and reappear at the finger-tips, one after the other—snap, snap, snap, snap?"

"What has that got to do—"

"Whenever you saw me, you'd beg to know how it was done. 'Please,' you said. 'I'll be your slave for a year,' you said. You'd whine. You'd pout."

"I was a kid, Edouard. I—"

"Maybe you could have handled that trick technically, I don't know for certain. But you lacked something very essential. You lacked the history, the experience. Do you recall what Houdini once said? 'I do nothing a child couldn't do—with twenty years of practice.' There was great wisdom in that."

I worked on a one-handed shuffle that had been giving me trouble.

"I'm simply asking you to accept that while I have nothing but respect and admiration for you, you don't have the years under your belt—certainly not the right years—to get involved in the private intrigues of a small group of very old men. It was all so long ago."

"It can't be all that deeply buried if—"

"Paul, you must listen to me." Clément's voice took on a quiet force. "Josef is gone. I know that you think you're doing something very splendid in his memory, but it won't change matters. I suspect that even your considerable magic skills cannot bring him back from the dead."

"That's not fair, Edouard. I—"

Nussbaum appeared in the doorway wearing a snug-fitting powder-blue tux. The accents over the pockets angled upward like wing flaps, and the ruffles on his maroon shirt looked about two inches deep. "I'm a little nervous," he said. "How do I look?"

"Great," Clément said.

"Snappy," I agreed.

"In this business," Nussbaum said, "you gotta dress sharp." He tried to smooth his lapels. "I think I'm gonna give them a few minutes of the dove act. What do you think? Just the highlights. Like I did last week at the library show. Stick with tradition, huh? They liked the doves well enough thirty years ago."

"A fine idea," Clément said.

"Absolutely," I confirmed.

"Thanks, guys," Nussbaum said. He opened the refrigerator and reached for a carton of milk.

I started to ask another of my clever and penetrating questions, but Clément cut me off. "Paul," he said, "are you certain you won't change your mind and accompany us to the audition? I'm sure Jacob would love to have you along."

It was a cheap shot and Clément knew it. Nussbaum

103

turned from the refrigerator with a hopeful look on his face. "Yeah," he said, "it might really impress those producers if they thought I was a old friend of yours."

"I'd like to go, Jacob," I said, "but I can't. As I was telling Edouard, who must not have heard me, I have to move my stuff out of my apartment by noon tomorrow or—"

"That's quite all right, Paul," Clément said. "We understand that you have important things to do. More important, certainly"—he gave me a meaningful glance—"than following a couple of old magicians around, listening to them ramble on about the old days. . . ."


The sound stage for the *Magic Cavalcade* reunion was out in Queens. I think the cab driver took a couple of wrong turns on the way to jack up the fare, but I couldn't be sure, given my dim understanding of the terrain. I got past the guard at the door by flashing my green Society of American Magicians membership card, which impressed him mightily for some reason. Clément and Nussbaum had studio passes.

The shooting floor was larger by half than the one where we tape the Stain Begone commercials, and about four times busier. I counted a dozen small setups and rehearsal stages scattered through the room at odd angles, so that lighting and backdrops could be shared. Scrim panels and duct tape gave the place a slapped-together atmosphere, and I couldn't detect any reason for most of the black cables that snaked across the floor, except to trip people. Somewhere in the background a drill press added to the general din.

On a large platform at the rear of the studio, a team of stage carpenters worked to re-create the *Magic Cavalcade* set, which had been an unholy coupling of Egyptology and Bauhaus. A cardboard obelisk and a Styrofoam pyramid stood at the foot of the stage, ready for deployment. The original design had been loosely patterned on Maskelyne and Devant's Egyptian Hall—England's "Home of Mystery"—which had been bombed out in 1944. The half-constructed set did something strange to my memory. I turned away quickly.

A small, athletic-looking woman with short black hair hurried toward me. "Mr. Galliard," she called, "it's me, Mindy—"

"Kramer," I said. "Mindy Kramer. I recognize your voice from my answering machine."

"That's right," she said. "I have called a few times. Well, have you reconsidered our offer of a spot on the program? We'd even let you close the show, if you wanted."

"No," I said. "I'm just here lending moral support to a friend."

"Oh dear," she said. "When I saw you standing there in your costume, I just assumed—wait just a minute. Don't you move." She hurried away and reappeared a moment later dragging a man by the arm. He was about my age or younger, bearded, and wore blue jeans and a red plaid lumberjack shirt. I felt certain he wasn't really a lumberjack.

"Mr. Galliard," Mindy said, "I'd like you to meet the director of our extravaganza, Sutton Forrester. We all call him Chip." Forrester and I shook hands while Mindy gave an approving nod at how well we were getting along. "Chip has been just dying to meet you, Mr. Galliard. He talks about you all the time."

"Good to meet you," the director said, containing his enthusiasm nicely.

"I was just telling Mr. Galliard how much we'd like to have him on the show," Mindy said. "I know it would just make the program."

"It *would* be good," Forrester admitted. "You going to do it?"

"No," I said.

"I'll take that as a maybe," Forrester said as he walked away.

Mindy followed me over to the coffee urn where Clément and Nussbaum stood. "Well now," she said, "which one of you is Mr. Nussbaum?" Both men were roughly three times her age, but she spoke as if inviting a grade schooler to display his insect collection.

"The one on the left is Nussbaum," I said. "In the tuxedo."

"Are you all ready, Mr. Nussbaum? Would you like to run through your tricks for us?"

Nussbaum ran his hands over his lapels and pockets, checking the placement of his props. Then he shuffled over to the small rehearsal platform Mindy had indicated. I watched him go and then turned back to look at Clément.

Over the years, I'd formed some comfortable notions about my elderly magician friends. They were like exhibits in a favorite museum that I could visit at my convenience and not think about much afterward. Just as I'd expected them to understand that I was no longer a child, I found myself having to accept rather suddenly that they were a good deal more than what they seemed.

Nussbaum took his place beside a small fringed drop-well table, smiling broadly at a nonexistent audience. Sutton Forrester, the boy-director, had to be prompted to look up from his clipboard.

The old magician cleared his throat, straining to be heard above the undiminished hubbub of construction. "Thank you for your kind reception, my friends," he said. "As it is a bit warm in here, I do not suppose I'll be needing these. . . ." Nussbaum tossed his white gloves into the air, transforming them into a white dove that fluttered its way to the floor. Mindy gave a game round of applause. Forrester looked down at his clipboard.

I edged up behind Clément. "Schneider dead of poison," I said in a quiet voice, as if ticking off a laundry list.

From the stage, Nussbaum said, "I take a colorful silken handkerchief . . ."

"The evidence destroyed in my apartment," I said to the back of Clément's head. He didn't move. I may as well have been begging for the secret of the four-ace trick.

**106**

"And voilà! Another lovely dove appears! Let us place it here in this cage."

"Now you and Nussbaum, who never really cared for each other, cling together like Hippety-Hop Rabbits. Why? Fear? Desperation? Mutual distrust?"

"Here I hold an empty cloth sack. Is it possible that still another live dove may appear from within its folds?"

"What was Schneider trying to say when he died? 'Red cats'? What does that mean?"

"Yes! It is possible! Another dove has magically appeared!"

I was getting nowhere with Clément, but I figured I might do better with Nussbaum. I let my eyes drift to the small platform where Nussbaum was valiantly staging his act for the uninterested director.

I'd seen Nussbaum's dove routine maybe three hundred times in the last twenty years, and he never varied it by an inch or a line. "It's a halfway decent dove act," he'd always said. "Why tamper?"

I started mouthing the patter to myself. *Let us put this dove, too, into the large cage.*

"Let us put this dove, too, into the large cage," Nussbaum said, covering a moment's fumbling as the dove flapped and tried to get free.

*Then we shall cover the cage with this cloth, and lift it up like so.*

"Then we shall cover the cage with this cloth, and lift it up like so." Nussbaum carried the cloth-covered cage a few steps forward.

*And hey presto! In a flash of fire, the dove cage miraculously disappears!*

Nussbaum never got that far. On the words "hey presto!" a loud crackling sound rippled across the soundstage and the black cloth in his hands erupted in a flash of fire larger than any I'd ever seen—so large that for a moment Nussbaum appeared to embrace a brilliant orange column of flame.

I was halfway to the platform before I heard the first

screams. Nussbaum dropped onto his back and frantically kicked his legs a couple of times. Then he slapped at the flames on his chest. Then he died. I got there just in time to see that. I wish I'd been a little slower.

I knelt down and wrapped my coat around a wet and blackened form that had once been a kindly old man with a halfway decent dove act. There wasn't much else to do. Two cameramen, one with a fire blanket, the other with an extinguisher, stood over us helplessly. One of them had a white feather stuck in his hair. I looked past them. I was looking for Clément.

He came up slowly on unsteady legs. The quiet composure he'd shown five minutes earlier was gone.

"I think," I said to him, "it's time you gave away some secrets."

# Chapter 10

I was getting to be an old hand at filing police statements. Clément and I had spent hours at a precinct house in Queens, answering questions and making arrangements for Nussbaum's remains. It was late evening by the time we got back to Manhattan. Clément wanted a strong cup of coffee, and I happened to have the keys to a coffee shop.

Frieda's place had been closed for several hours. I managed to get past the security gratings and shut down the alarm system without too much trouble. Working the espresso maker proved more difficult.

All the chairs in the shop were still upended on top of the tables after the last sweeping of the day. Clément took a couple down while I toiled behind the counter. I couldn't find the overhead light switches, so the only illumination in the place came from a desk lamp near the cash register. Clément looked very small and frail sitting by himself in the shadows.

"I still don't believe it," he said. "After all of these years. I'd started to hope the whole thing would go away. I was beginning to forget."

I scooped up some ground coffee in a small filter basket and fitted it into the moorings of the machine. Then I flicked some switches and hoped for the best. I didn't say anything to Clément. He didn't need any prodding now.

"You must understand that I came into the matter quite late. Much of what I know of this business I learned secondhand. I barely knew the rest of them—Nussbaum, Schneider, your father—in Austria. That was before we were bound together by—by circumstances." Clément laid his hands on the table. The metal buckles on his arthritis braces glinted briefly in the dim light.

"I was quite a young man in 'thirty-seven and 'thirty-eight, but I could see what was happening in the world." He looked at me. "You're aware this was a troubled time in Europe?"

I nodded, indicating that I'd heard something of the kind.

"It took no particular genius to see these things, only a suspension of disbelief. For a magician, this was not difficult. The reason so many people stayed behind is that they simply refused to accept what their eyes and ears were telling them. It couldn't be happening, they said. Me, I made my living at things that couldn't happen. Such matters were my stock-in-trade."

He sighed and looked around the empty shop. "I attended political meetings; grew outspoken. Soon it became necessary for me to leave Austria. I joined the Vichy forces, but I was not satisfied to be a foot soldier. I wished to do more."

The espresso maker began making loud noises. Clément looked up eagerly. "Do you suppose I might have some of that coffee now?" he asked. I got up and looked for some cups. Clément kept on talking. I honestly think he would have talked on if he'd been alone in the shop.

"All the time I entertained the other soldiers with my magic tricks. Even with the war I wanted to keep in practice, and the men seemed to enjoy it. Sometimes at night they would come around to ask for this trick or that

**110**

one. . . ." He smiled, remembering. "I would even bring cards and coins along with me on maneuvers, just in case."

Clément murmured a thank-you as I handed him a cup of something very much like coffee.

"One day a message I received. From our captain. He wished to see me immediately about these magic tricks. Naturally I did not look forward to this. I expected a reprimand, although many officers enjoyed my tricks too." He paused and sipped the coffee, grimacing slightly.

"When I came to the office, there was another man there with our captain. A small man with flaming red hair. He did not wear a uniform, but I sensed that he was powerful. The captain seemed to defer to him.

"The man had many questions for me. He asks, You are a German? No, I say, I am Austrian. My father was a Swiss. But you could pass? Perhaps, I say. Have you ever been to Germany? Many times, before the war. This seems to please him. Then he asks, You are a Jew? My mother, I answer. I have nothing to hide. He looks at me very carefully. A *mischling*, he says. You don't look it. That is good. One more question, do you have a wife?" Clément set down his coffee cup and leaned back in his chair, fixing his eyes on the ceiling. "Do you have a wife? This is when I began to know what was happening. There were other more serious questions—questions about politics, about education—but already I have a good idea what is happening. And the red-haired man, he saw that I knew, and he gave a terrible smile, a cold smile. That was my first experience with Horst Katzenbacher."

"Ho-Ho?" I asked, speaking for the first time since we entered the shop. "The recruiter was Ho-Ho?"

Clément took another sip of coffee. "Ho-Ho, as you call him, was a clever, powerful, and ruthless man. I learned that very quickly."

"What exactly did he want you to do?"

"He wanted me to join his circus. We were to entertain the troops."

"That's it?"

"The German troops."

"Ah."

"Katzenbacher had influence with someone or other connected with a propaganda minister. It began that way. I was just another performer. A flame swallower. That was the beauty of it; we really were what we seemed to be. The Germans saw only a third-rate group of magicians. Not as popular as the singers and dancers, but certainly preferable to the opera company. And if our tricks failed to spark the interest, one could always admire the assistants in their revealing costumes. Katzenbacher's circus was much in demand, I assure you. To the British, however, we were something very different."

"You worked for the British? MI Six?"

He looked at me with raised eyebrows. "That would appeal to you, wouldn't it? But no. We had no official sanction. We simply did our magic show. However, if in the course of our travels we happened to come across any information about where a particular regiment was bound for the next day, well, we had friends in England who found the knowledge useful."

I got up to pour him some more coffee. I had a hundred urgent questions, but I felt the need to proceed cautiously, afraid that once the shock of Nussbaum's death wore off, Clément would retreat into his former silence.

"Edouard," I said carefully, "you're Jewish. Full-blooded or not, it was enough for the Germans. Weren't you and the others running an absurd risk?"

A pained expression passed over his face. "As it happens," he said, "removing my stage makeup was the most dangerous thing I did during the war, and I did it seldom. Understand, though, that we spent almost no time at all in Germany. Most of our work was in France and other occupied countries. As to the other risks, they were small. Katzenbacher had recruited carefully. Each of us had a skill that he needed for his operations. No one person took on too much of the burden at once. Jacob wasn't even working as a magician when they found him. He was an engraver. Did you know that? It proved useful to our associates in the Resistance. He became a notorious forger. He could do anything. Vichy internal travel passes, German industrial papers—anything at all."

"And my father? What did he do while all this was going on?

"Several things. First of all, he was the only one of us who had any fame in Germany before the war. His presence on the bill gave Katzenbacher's circus a credibility it would otherwise have lacked. That's why Katzenbacher needed him. It may have been what gave him the idea in the first place; the two of them had been friends in Stuttgart."

"That was my father's contribution, then? Name recognition?"

"Hardly. I doubt that you ever knew this, but Galliard—that wasn't his name in those days, of course— he had an unusual mind. A wonderful memory. That, I believe, was what attracted him to magic. You've heard of the British performer at the turn of the century? Datas?"

"The Memory Man?"

"Exactly. I won't say that your father was that good, but almost. The audience could ask him anything: dates in history, questions about sporting events, the price of eggs in China. It was all stored in his wonderful memory. It made for a sensational act, I can tell you. He always amazed them. And he could absorb anything at a glance. That made him useful to Katz. And it—"

"Katzenbacher, you mean?"

"Yes, I suppose so. 'Katz' was what he called himself later. In America. He had many names before that. It was necessary, in the circumstances. He found that—what is it, Paul? You look so startled all of a sudden."

"Red cats," I said.

"Yes," Clément said. "I wondered when you would see that."

"Schneider's dying words to the kids at that birthday party. He was talking about Ho-Ho."

"Ho-Ho was your name for him. A child's nickname. We called him Red, because of his hair."

I stood up and walked to the front window of the shop. My throat felt tight and there was an insistent buzzing in my ears. I got that sensation whenever something happened that seemed way out of whack. The first time I'd noticed it was after I'd turned in a midterm in which I'd confused General Longstreet with one of his lesser-known cousins. It starts at the base of my neck and spreads all the way to my forehead, centering in my ears. It's something that Spider-man and I have in common.

"Edouard," I said, "forgive me. I'm not my father's son. I can't absorb huge amounts of information at a glance. Not if I want to make sense of it, anyway. I've waited a long time to hear all this about Katzenbacher's circus, and I want to hear more. But right this second I don't see the connection between your war record and Schneider's death. Or Nussbaum's. These aren't exactly current events you've been telling me about. Years have passed. I can't believe that Schneider's final thoughts were of an old war buddy."

I turned away from the window. Clément's discomfort was plain in his features.

"Come on, Edouard," I said. "There must be some more urgent reason that Schneider died with Katzenbacher's name on his lips."

Clément's shoulders sagged. He looked down at his coffee cup and then up at the ceiling. When he spoke, his voice had grown very quiet. "You must understand," he said. "We were soldiers. Heroes. Enough time has passed so that I can properly say so. I am proud of what I did. Proud. But when I came to America after the war, I wanted only to be a magician. The others had the same idea. The rest of it, that was behind us. Katz, he had never been a magician to begin with. For a time he stayed in Europe.

**114**

He returned to Germany and had dealings on the black market in Frankfurt. American cigarettes, mostly. Also flour and chocolate."

Clément sat back and fingered the silver knob of his walking stick. "It was not such a good idea for Katz to return to Germany. He made enemies. Many enemies. After only a short time he came to join the rest of us in America. He did not like the new life here. He was used to being in command, and needed something useful to do. For a time we let him manage us. That was our mistake, though I must admit he did a fine job in the beginning. It was he who was largely responsible for our success on *Magic Cavalcade*. But Katz was not satisfied only to manage a group of magicians. Still he wanted to be something more than he seemed on the surface."

"I don't get it," I said. "He continued to report troop movements to British intelligence?"

Clément favored me with a weak smile. "He traveled frequently to Europe. There he continued his dealings on the black market. This went on for some time, I understand, though we did not learn the true extent of it until it was too late."

"Too late?"

Clément continued to finger his walking stick, inspecting the tip for signs of wear. "In time Katz's activities began to attract unwanted attention. It began with immigration officials, but quickly grew more serious. Soon it became clear that he would be extradicted."

"Where?"

"West Germany."

"Why?"

"War crimes."

"Wait a minute. You just got through telling me—"

"I did not lie. Katz was many evil things, but he was not a Nazi." Clément carefully laid his walking stick on the table. "You have heard, perhaps, of Aktion Suehnezeichen?"

I shook my head.

**115**

"After the war the West Germans grew eager to make reparations. Or at least they wished to give that impression. Many trials were held. Many sentences passed. Katz had made powerful enemies in that country, as I said. They had tried to prosecute him for the crimes he actually did commit, and they had failed. Collaboration, on the other hand, was more easily proven."

"But Katz—"

"Katz had dealings with German officers during the war. We all did, but most especially Katz. It was the nature of what we did, the very thing that made us useful to the British. But after the war the West Germans saw this as an opportunity. They planned to prosecute Katz as some sort of double agent. No doubt they would have, if matters had ever gotten to that point."

"But they didn't?"

"No. Katz did what he always did. He struck a bargain. His freedom in exchange for a halt to his activities. This did not entirely satisfy his accusers, however. They wanted a collaborator." Clément folded his hands and rubbed them gingerly. "Once again Katz offered a solution."

"What was that?"

"One of us. We were public figures, to an extent. More visible, in any case, than Katz ever was. Surely it would prove most impressive if a famous magician, a magician appearing on American television no less, were to be exposed as a war criminal by the West Germans themselves. It seems outlandish now, does it not? But the possibility appeared very real at the time. I did not know then that Katz was the betrayer. I would not know that for many years. I only knew enough then to become frightened. Very frightened. We braced ourselves for the worst."

I had been pacing in front of the window. I stopped and fixed my eyes on something in the street. "But the accusation never came, did it?"

"No," he said softly.

"Tell me something. My father's death. It wasn't an accident, was it?"

"Paul," he said. "Forgive me. I do not know.'

The buzzing in my ears got louder.

# Chapter 11

I put Clément in a cab and went back into the pastry shop, figuring I'd sack out upstairs. Though I still thought of the apartment above the shop as belonging exclusively to Schneider, Frieda and I had worked out the terms of my stewardship earlier in the week. I hadn't moved any of my things over yet, but I was beat, and even though sleep seemed only a remote possibility, I didn't feel like going back uptown to my old place.

I went to the pay phone in the corner of the shop and called the brand new answering machine I'd bought that morning. After only three tries I got the beeperless remote to play back the message tape. There were four messages from Clara, each one more urgent than the last. I fished out my pocket watch. It was after midnight. Clara's most recent message had been left only twenty minutes earlier. I dropped some more change into the phone and dialed.

She answered on the first ring. "Are you all right?" she asked after I'd said hello. "I was in the newsroom when the report came in. It must have been awful."

"It was," I said.

"Where are you?"

"Frieda's. My friend Clément and I have been talking about old times."

"Hang on. Stay right there. I'll be there in half an hour."

"Really? Gracious. What's all this about?"

"Nothing. Something. Just hang on. Buy yourself a cup of coffee."

I closed my eyes and massaged the bridge of my nose "Listen, kid, I don't mean to be rude, but I'm a little worn out, what with tales of the Resistance and my friends catching fire and all. Couldn't this wait until morning?"

"It's important, Paul. Forget the coffee. Go across the street and get yourself a stiff drink at the Tin Tavern. You'll need it. I'll meet you there."

I knew there wasn't much point in arguing. "Maybe I'd better grab a cab to my apartment and change," I said. "I've been stuck in my working clothes all day."

"Don't worry about it. You're a dream in black. Especially when you wear that snappy paisley vest with all the glitter. Just go across the street and wait for me."

"Clara, what's the deal here? You—"

"See you in half an hour." She hung up.


The Tin Tavern had gone neon since the last time I'd been in. I sat down at the bar next to a guy whose hair looked like a green abatis. Nobody seemed to notice my opera cape.

Clara showed about twenty minutes later. She had a flat metal film can tucked under her arm.

"Evening, ma'am," I said, doffing my top hat. "Can I interest you in a Rob Roy? I've been conducting an informal survey of out-of-date cocktails. This one was last seen, I believe, in *After the Thin Man*, starring Myrna Loy and William Powell. Both the movie and the drink have held up well, I find."

"Absolut on the rocks, please," Clara said to the bartender. She slid the film can onto the bar.

"What do you have in there?" I asked. "Home movies?" She didn't answer.

"Who's looking after Franklin while you're traipsing about at midnight, may I ask?"

"My sister," she said distractedly. She drummed her fingers on top of the can. "Paul, I don't know exactly how to approach this. I was doing some thinking about all this business and about what you said about your father—"

"Look. I'm sorry we ever got into that last night. It's not really your problem and I don't expect you to—"

"—so I spent the day digging around in the archives of the Museum of Broadcasting. I have special industry access, you know."

"My," I said.

"I wanted to see what I could find out about the original *Magic Cavalcade*. I don't know, after what you said last night, I had this awful feeling that you might decide to catch bullets on that anniversary program after all. Who knows what crazy ideas you might have about 'finding yourself,' or coming to terms with your father's accident, or any of that kind of crap."

I didn't say anything.

"Well." All business, Clara flipped open a small steno pad and put on a pair of red, round-rimmed reading glasses. "*Magic Cavalcade* first aired on a Sunday, June 24, 1956. It stayed in that time slot for three weeks before shifting to Tuesday, also at seven, where it remained for three years. The show broadcast live and had an hour-long format featuring five magicians, many of them regulars, in segments running six to eight minutes each. The segments were linked by an emcee named Marcus McGruder and his wisecracking puppet, Binky."

"McGruder was a nice guy," I said. "He died a few months back. Binky was inconsolable."

"Among the most popular of the *Magic Cavalcade* performers was one Thomas J. Galliard, a recent immigrant. Contemporary newspapers lauded his stage style as 'light and breezy.' Galliard, according to the notes on his audition forms, was favored by the producers since he'd managed, unlike many of his friends, to divest himself of the Germanic accent he'd brought with him from Austria. German accents were still unpopular at the time."

"He was quite good with voices and accents, now that I think of it. One of my only really clear memories of him is of a folk story he used to tell with lots of talking animals in it. He did all the different voices."

Clara took a sip of her drink, apparently waiting for me to go on.

"That's it," I said. "Not much of a story, I know, but then he wasn't much of a father."

"One night, as you know, Galliard decided to stage the bullet-catch trick made famous—or infamous—by the death of Chung Ling Soo forty years earlier. And so, one night—"

"May 26, 1959."

She took another pull on her drink, looking at me over her glasses. "And so," she continued, "on May 26, 1959, Galliard met his accidental—albeit tragic—death. I underscore the word 'accidental.' "

"A week ago I would have agreed with you. The stuff I was telling you last night? About my father's wands? I'd written those off a long time ago. I always assumed some souvenir hunter had snagged them. And as for Ho-Ho getting beaten up that night, let's just say it doesn't fry the imagination. But then—"

"I know, I know. You found that broken wand in Schneider's drawer."

"Nussbaum got one too. And Clément. He's scared half out of his mind." I gave her a scaled-back version of what Clement had told me earlier.

By the time I finished, she'd resumed drumming her fingers across the top of the film can. "That doesn't make what I have to tell you any easier," she said.

Clara, after all I've seen and heard tonight, not much would shock me."

"Ever heard of a kinescope?"

"Sure, it's where—it's when—you've got to be kidding me. Tell me you're kidding."

"Paul, it was almost S.O.P. in those days. Standard operating procedure. Why do you think all these newly discovered episodes of old live comedies keep turning up? During most live broadcasts in the fifties, especially those on the Dumont network, a specially synchronized film camera was kept rolling on a television monitor, providing a film record of the broadcast. Hundreds of these were promptly lost, misfiled, or destroyed. But a fair number survived."

"If this is a joke, it's not funny."

"It's not a joke and it's not funny." She pressed her hand flat on the film can. "This is a kinescope of *Magic Cavalcade* the night your father did the bullet catch. I found it after five hours of digging, in a box marked 'Magic Show.' If you don't want to watch this, I'll certainly understand. Frankly, when I found it I considered destroying the film myself. But then I thought, if you did see it, maybe it would convince you once and for all to forget about that damn trick, which I see no reason—"

"Have you watched it?"

"No, not yet."

I put some money on the bar. "Let's go," I said.

There's an all-night liquor store near Reel Thing Studios, where, if you're not too particular about brand names, you can find pretty much anything in convenient carry-along sizes. We picked up a pint of Scotch before crossing the street to the studio. I seem to recall that it was my idea.

We got buzzed through at the front entrance of the studio and signed in with the night watchman. Clara led me down a long corridor I'd never been in before, to a heavy metal door marked with the word STORAGE spelled

**123**

out in black electrical tape. Clara dug around in her straw shoulder bag and came up with a key hooked to a long wooden paddle.

"I got this from the production manager," she told me. "He promised to kill me, creatively, if I disturbed anything." She tried working the lock. "Can't seem to— the key doesn't seem to want to turn—"

I bent low over the lock. "Wrong key," I said.

"Great. That's typical. It happens constantly with the ladies' room key. It adds to the general air of urgency around here."

"Would the night-desk guy have a duplicate?"

"No. They're very territorial about their keys around here. Access to equipment is a sign of power." She stared at the heavy metal door. "Maybe it's fate, Galliard. A golden opportunity for you to back out."

"I can pick it," I said.

"You can what?"

"I can pick it. The lock."

"Oh, come on! With what? A hairpin? I don't even wear hairpins."

I sighed as I reached into my pocket for my kit. "Nobody ever really picked a lock with a hairpin. It's just not that simple. You need a lock-pick set. I've got a big kit at home, but this usually does the job in a pinch."

"That? A pen?"

"Observe. I unscrew the barrel and what do we see inside? Lock picks! The pen clip doubles as a tension tool."

"A what?"

"A tension tool. Look. You stick it in the keyhole like this and turn it slightly until you feel a bite. That way, as each pin in the lock is raised to the shear line, the tension keeps it from falling back down into the core."

She just stared at me.

"Sometimes you can rake a lock just by pulling a pick across the pins. That won't work here."

"How do you know?"

"This is a pretty serious old tumbler lock. Maybe even a little rusty inside. I'll have to do it one pin at a time." I had five picks with me, and I could tell at a glance that I'd need the half-diamond-shaped one to do the job, but I made a little show of holding each one up to the lock, like an artist selecting the proper brush. I'm a ham, no matter what the circumstances.

"Where do you get your hands on something like that?" Clara asked. "They look like tiny dental tools."

"I mail-ordered it from a guy named Rex Streenburger in Omaha. He's a locksmith." I began probing the lock with the half-diamond pick. "Old Rex is very careful to specify in his brochure that he sells only to accredited locksmiths, but I've never known him to ask for anyone's papers."

"What possessed you to send for them in the first place?"

"A few years back I had an idea of myself as the next great escape artist. I took apart a few locks, learned the basics." I felt the lock's inner plug turn slightly as the first driver pin gave way. "Not much ever came of it, although I'm the first person my friends call when they're locked out of their apartments."

"I suppose it's occurred to you that you'd make a fairly good second-story man."

"Maybe," I said. "Maybe then I could have stayed in graduate school." I stood up and pushed open the door.

A light switch just inside the door illuminated three bare bulbs hanging from the ceiling in extension sockets. A half flight of stairs led down into a dank and windowless room filled mostly with old scenery panels stacked one against the other. Metal bookcases lined two walls, their shelves stacked with silver film cans. A pair of scarred wooden tables held every manner of outdated film equipment, including an ancient film-splicing setup, several projectors with loose springs hanging out, a black cloth changing bag for reloading film magazines, and something that might have been a prototype developer. In a far corner stood a gray metal optical reader which looked as if it hadn't been touched in years. Clara headed for it.

"You know how to run that thing?" I asked.

She nodded. "My alma mater wasn't exactly up to the minute when it came to video technology. We considered this state of the art."

The machine had two-foot-long spindles mounted on either side of a short track of sprockets and a tiny viewing screen. Each spindle had a weighted crank on the end.

Clara threw her coat over the take-up reel of a rusted projector and pulled on a pair of white gloves.

"I never knew you were a debutante," I said.

"Cotton gloves," she said. "So I won't smudge the emulsion." She peeled off the tape that sealed the film can shut and lifted out the reel. "I have a spare bulb with me in case the one in the viewer is burned out. It was working three months ago, though. I used it to look through some old file footage."

I took off my cape and top hat and found two of those metal-banded wood-topped stools that seem to exist only around electrical equipment.

Clara clicked a toggle switch on the viewer to no apparent effect. "Check the plug, okay?"

I did, crawling through three inches of dust to reach it. "Anything?" I called.

"No . . . wait. Okay, we're cooking now." She mounted the reel on the left-hand spindle and threaded the leader through the sprockets and into the right-hand take-up reel.

"We're ready to go," she said. "Are you sure you know what you're doing? Do you realize what you're about to see? Have you really thought it through?"

"I'm determined not to think it through," I said. "I just want to see the film. Maybe it's got something to do with Schneider and Nussbaum and Clément, maybe not. Maybe I just want to look the albatross in the eye. Hell, plenty of people have to watch their parents die. I'm just getting to it a little late. As usual."

"But—"

"If we spend enough time talking about it, I'm sure we'll come up with dozens of convincing reasons to take the film and throw it from a bridge. I know that. But for now let's just watch it."

Clara walked to the door and flicked off the overhead lights so that the only illumination in the room came from the view screen of the optical reader. Then she began turning the right-hand crank that pulled film through the machine, keeping her left hand on the film reel to act as a brake. The view screen itself couldn't have been more than three inches square, so we had to pull our stools up close and hunch over to get a good look.

A few seconds of Academy leader markings flashed across the tiny screen, then the program began as a series of title cards appeared. They were written in ornate script on what appeared to be heavy cardboard and were sitting on an easel in front of a stage curtain. The cards changed every few seconds, trumpeted by a little puff of smoke that did little to disguise the clunky stop-action photography. After the final card disappeared, the curtain behind the easel parted.

What I saw next had the quality of opening an old photo album or stumbling across some once-cherished rag doll. In childhood I had seen *Magic Cavalcade* dozens of times—whenever my mother let me stay up late—but I hadn't expected the memory of it to be so sharp. Earlier in the day I'd stood on a faithful reproduction of the set, but the flickering black-and-white image on the view screen came far nearer to what I actually remembered.

"Any sound?" I asked.

"No. You mind?"

"Not terribly. That's McGruder," I said, "and the gentleman on his arm is Binky. Can you speed this up? My father was last on the bill that night."

She cranked the film through faster so the images on the screen passed in accelerated motion.

"I don't recognize that first guy," I said. "Looks like

**127**

a reasonably good sleight-of-hand act, though. Here's a few words from our sponsor ... there's McGruder again —hey! Wait! I'll be damned, there's Nussbaum!"

Clara slowed the film to near-normal speed. "Look," I said, "he's doing the exact same dove act. If this thing had any sound, he'd be saying, 'And voilà! Another lovely dove appears! Let us place it here in this cage.' "

I stared at the image of the man not yet old, frightened, or dead. "All right, there's his big finale. You can speed it up again. Wait a minute. Boy, this is quite a night. That's Clément."

"That's Clément?" Clara asked. "Quite a hairstyle."

"Isn't it, though? He once told me he'd hoped to look like 'that young fellow with the guitar.' "

I watched the figure on the screen with fascination. The camera had Clément in a medium close-up as he went through some card manipulations with an oversize deck. He did some peel-away fans and an especially good vanish of the entire deck, only to reproduce it from behind the head of an underdressed assistant. He finished up with an impressive card spread and turnover. I tried to imagine how he'd felt when arthritis first stiffened his fingers.

Clara sped up to get through some more commercials. "You know," she said, "it's really quite beautiful, some of it. Those card tricks especially. It's very graceful. Almost balletic."

"Gosh, Clara. That's really vivid."

"All right, all right. Who's this next guy?"

"That's Schneider."

She hunched closer to the view screen. "So that's Schneider, huh?"

"That's him."

"He's nice-looking. I mean nice-kind more than nice-handsome."

"He was nice-looking."

"What's he doing? He's just standing there."

"A mentalism effect. You see the way they keep cutting

to the audience? Schneider is taking questions, doing some mind-reading warm-ups. See? Here comes the blindfold. He'll go down into the audience and call off serial numbers from dollar bills." An assistant fastened a black cloth over Schneider's eyes and led him toward the edge of the stage. He hesitated a bit, taking her arm much the same way he would take mine years later when I helped him up stairs or over curbs.

"Speed it up, okay?"

"Really? I thought you'd want to see this."

"Just speed it up."

I didn't recognize the fourth magician, but he seemed to be doing a pretty fair illusion act capped off with the inevitable Sawed Lady routine. Clara slowed the film down when McGruder and Binky reappeared.

"See how they've had to close the curtains after each act to give the stagehands time to set up for the next guy? They actually brought off five magic routines in an hour. Broadcast live. It boggles the mind. These days you—"

I broke off when the curtains parted to show the stage nearly empty except for a large sheet of glass mounted on a metal tripod. A man I recognized more from photographs than life strode onto the stage, displaying his palms in response to what must have been a round of applause. He stood addressing the camera for a few moments. I assumed he was doing a big buildup, explaining the history and dangers of the effect he was about to perform.

"He sort of looks like you," Clara said quietly. "The eyes and the mouth. There's something about the way he holds himself too. I can't quite explain it."

I didn't respond. I watched as my father summoned a boyish Officer Chasfield, the NYPD's star marksman, from the audience and motioned for another round of applause. Chasfield looked pale and slight next to my father, and he kept nervously running his hands over his dark crewcut.

After giving the policeman a few instructions, my father carefully demonstrated the workings of the rifle that, in a few moments, would end his life. Chasfield seemed horribly tense, actually dropping the bullet at one point. My father, by contrast, looked almost serene.

When I was about thirteen years old I became obsessed with the idea of making flashes of fire appear from my hands. After some unsuccessful experiments with flash paper, I paid seven dollars for a device called the "fingertip flashpot," a flesh-colored cylinder with a spring arm that touched off a small charge of gunpowder. Practicing at home in front of the hall mirror one day, I managed to block the barrel opening with my index finger just as the charge went off. It charred my finger black and stung like hell, but I remember that my first thought was not of the pain. My first thought was despair over a trick gone bad. Many times in the years since, I've wondered how my father felt in that fraction of an instant when he saw the rifle barrel flash and felt the hot sting in his chest. Were his last thoughts of pain and dying, or of a trick gone bad?

On the view screen my father pulled out a handkerchief and wiped his face, placing it back in his pocket after coughing once. Then he put on a pair of heavy gloves, using his teeth to get a grip on the second one.

I felt the old buzzing start in my ears. "I don't believe this," I said.

"Want to stop?"

"No, no. It's just that—no."

The two men—Chasfield and my father—took up positions on opposite sides of the stage. My father stood behind the sheet of glass and raised his gloved hands to protect his face from shards. Then, without any great fanfare, the gun fired, the glass shattered, and my father collapsed in a heap. One arm slapped the stage as his body twisted away from the camera. Despite the absence of sound, I could sense the pandemonium as figures poured from the wings and surrounded my father. After a few seconds the camera panned down to the stage floor and remained there, lingering on a cigarette butt.

Clara stopped cranking the film and we sat for a long time.

"You all right?" she asked after a while.

I grunted, eloquently.

"You look as if you've seen a ghost. Sorry—I guess you have."

"I wish it were that simple."

"Simple?"

I clicked off the view screen, plunging the room into total darkness. We sat there some more. It had to be two or three in the morning, but we sat there. I had something to tell her. Something very important. Instead I took out the pint of Scotch we'd bought, twisted off the cap and took a long swallow.

We were still sitting there when the morning crew came in.

# Chapter 12

It had been a busy three days. I'd finally tracked down Michael, my itinerant roommate, and broken the unhappy news about our apartment fire. I'd finished taping the Stain Begone commercial I'd failed to complete earlier in the week, and moved my furniture, my magic equipment, and my rabbit and doves over to Schneider's place. Also, I'd signed on to be shot in thirty-six hours.

By the day before the broadcast most of the smaller camera setups and rehearsal areas had disappeared from the *Magic Cavalcade* soundstage, replaced by rows of seats that would be filled with an audience the following night. Boy-Director Sutton "Chip" Forrester and I sat in the front row of seats, ironing out the particulars of the bullet-catch effect. I wanted to be sure Forrester understood the details. He seemed to have more important things on his mind.

"Where will the camera be at the start of my segment?" I asked him.

"Huh?" he said.

"The camera, where will it be?"

"Oh. Well, I'm sure there'll be at least three cameras, depending on the close-up angles."

"Sutton. Chip. We've been all through this. You promised you'd use only one camera. No cuts, no breaks. When this is all over, I don't want people accusing me of trick photography. I hate that. It's why magic doesn't work on TV most of the time. It looks faked, even when it isn't. I don't let them do much cutting even on those Stain Begone ads. Not when I'm doing a trick, anyway."

Forrester managed to look interested. "Right. Sorry, Paul. I've got a lot on my mind. We're grateful you changed your mind about coming on the show, but it's made for a hell of a lot of last-minute scrambling. I don't know how we're going to pull this together in time." He looked at me. "What did make you change your mind, anyway?"

"Your winning ways."

"Uh-huh. Whatever. It's just that I've got my camera guys screaming for a final shot list, the producer's breathing down my neck. It's a mess."

"Should we do this later, then?"

"What's that?"

"The walk-through. I came out here to walk through the effect, so you could see what happens when."

"Oh. Right. Let's do it now."

I climbed up onto a raised platform that had been constructed to suggest a proscenium stage. A number of cameramen, audio people, and other crew members milled about looking as if they didn't have too much to do. Some of them stood off in the wings behind the recently installed fire curtain. Others wandered around the stage examining the backdrops. Only one person—a teenage guy with a push broom—appeared to have any interest in what was going on.

I walked to the apron of the stage. "There are really just three key positions to keep track of," I told Forrester. "The first is where the shooter stands. That's right about here, stage left." I grabbed the guy with the push broom and dragged him over to the spot. "Right about there. Then we'll have the glass plate that the bullet gets fired through. That's position number two."

I ducked into the wings and grabbed a metal music stand. "That goes here, right of center. And finally there's me, the bold young magician. I'll be standing here, at position number three." I moved to far stage right, with my back against the fly curtains. "That okay for everyone?" The crew murmured their general approval.

I looked out into the seats. "Chip? These positions look all right to you?"

"Let's see. I wonder, can you be standing any more center when the gun goes off?"

"Not really."

"I guess it'll have to do, then. Mark it, Tom." Forrester made some pencil marks on a lucite clipboard in his lap while a gaffer hopped up on stage and marked the three spots with green tape. "Paul? Have you talked to that guy about firing the gun on the show? The police guy?"

"I've talked to him. He hasn't said yes or no yet."

"We haven't got a whole lot of time."

"I'll call him again this afternoon."

"Thanks. Now I want to see how this plays out, Paul. You mind taking us through it once? The blocking?"

"It's fairly simple," I said. I motioned to my stagehand friend. "Where's your broom?"

"Left it over there."

"Do you mind getting it? I promise I won't make you use it."

"That'll make a nice change," he said, trotting off to the wings.

"All right," I said. "The trick runs like this. First, I walk to the front here and say something stirring about the dark and haunting history of the bullet-catch effect. That'll last twenty or thirty seconds. Then I'll introduce our rifleman. He'll step forward, looking nervous and uncomfortable."

135

The stagehand reappeared and handed me the broom. "Stay here for a minute," I said. "You're a police lieutenant now."

"That's also a nice change."

"Have you got a name?"

"Henry."

"All right. Henry and I talk for a minute, establishing that he and I aren't in cahoots—yes?"

"No cahoots," said Henry.

"We also learn that he was once the star marksman of the New York Police Department. And although we don't mention it directly, we allude to the fact that this isn't the first time he's participated in a bullet-catching trick. Then we display the rifle. He makes a show of examining it to be certain it's in working order." I held out the broom.

"Nice," Henry said.

"Then, using a steel point that I provide, he scratches some markings onto the bullet."

"Excuse me," Forrester called from the seats. "Can I ask a question?"

"Please do." It moved me that he'd been paying such close attention.

"How close can we get on the marking of the bullet?"

"As close as you can. We want people to be sure there's no switch. The bullet they see loaded into the gun is the same one that'll show up later clenched between my teeth. I'll hold it up to the camera after he marks it, if you want."

"That'd be good."

"Got it. So I hold the marked bullet up to the camera, then I hand it to the lieutenant, who loads and cocks the gun. Next I lead the lieutenant to his spot and show him the glass plate, which will have some dramatic cross-hair markings on it to assist him in taking aim. Try it for us, Henry."

Henry raised the broom and sighted along the handle, squaring the bristles against his shoulder.

"Good. Then I walk over to my position on the other

side of the glass and give Henry his final instruction, which is to fire on command. Who have you got lined up as emcee, by the way?"

Forrester looked down at his clipboard. "Oh, let's see. The comic canceled. I got that guy—what's his name? The fat guy? Used to be on all the comedy revues in the fifties? With the great voice? Mitch Michaelson."

"Okay. We'll let him give the ready, aim, fire. But before he does, I'll say something clever but poignant to underscore what a brave fellow I am in the face of all this danger. Then I'll pull on my gloves and protective goggles and signal Michaelson to start the count. He can drag it out as much as he wants."

"Hold on a minute, Paul." Forrester had really perked up. "How tight can we get on the actual—you know—the actual shooting?"

"You mean how tight on me?"

"On you. Yeah."

"Come in as close as you want, I guess. But try not to miss all the flying glass. If you're going to go for a close-up, try to zoom in from the established shot rather than make a cut to a close-up camera."

"Why's that?"

"Chip—"

"Oh, right. Right. The trick-photography thing. Fine. Go on."

"Well, that's pretty much it. Henry fires the bullet, the glass plate at center stage shatters, I stagger backward for a second while the audience clutches their hearts. After an appropriately harrowing pause, I stride forward displaying the marked bullet between my teeth, and the skies ring with my praises. That do it for everyone?"

"Sounds good to me," said Henry, lowering his broom.

"There's one other thing I have to make clear," I said, deepening my voice a bit to suggest the gravity of the situation. "We can't have any extra people hanging around backstage while this is going on. Anybody who isn't essential will have to clear out. I'm not kidding. And under no circumstances can there be anyone standing behind me when the gun goes off. That's kind of important."

No one responded, but I could tell by the silence that I'd gotten the message across. I left the stage and answered a few questions for the stage manager, then I headed for a pay phone near the front entrance. Mindy Kramer, the assistant producer, intercepted me on the way. "Mr. Galliard?" she said. "Paul? I just want to—you know—say hi and thank you for changing your mind at the last minute like this. We could have gotten somebody else to do the bullet-catch thing, but it would have been kind of, I mean, noticeable. With you on it's like saying, 'It's cool,' you know?"

"Sure. Listen, would you just make sure that Chip was paying attention to what I said about the single camera shot? That he takes it seriously?"

"You bet. I know he seems a little, like, distracted, but it's because this is his first prime-time special and he's mondo nervous. He asked me to tell you that everybody's super-glad you'll be on the show  It just *makes* the program."

"Thanks," I said. "Were you able to track down that metal tripod that holds the glass plate?"

"Yeah, it was in the Museum of Magic, like you said. The guy on the phone was real nice. Where is Marshall, Michigan, anyway?"

"Near Tekonsha."

"He said he'd get his nephew to ship it out yesterday. It should get here today. But like I was saying, all of us connected with the show have, you know, kind of a creepy feeling about what happened back then—I mean, it was before I was even born or anything, but sometimes I think about it and I'm like—" She rolled her eyes and shoulders. "You know?"

"I know what you mean. Listen, did you order the glass for the stand?"

"Someone's picking it up this afternoon."

"Two sheets? One for dress rehearsal and one for the show?"

"That's what I told them, although I still don't see why we just couldn't have our guys here bang together a stand for you."

"Call it a deep respect for tradition."

She gave me a cut-the-crap smile. "What you mean is that the stand is part of the secret and you don't want anyone to find out about it."

I smiled back. "That's another way of looking at it."

"Well, it's good for the show, anyway. It's all part of the historical accuracy we want. It's like I was telling that reporter—"

"Reporter?"

"Yeah, from the paper. He's waiting for you in the lobby. Didn't I tell you?"

"Mindy, when I signed on to do the show, what did I say about press coverage?"

"I know you said you didn't want to have to do any interviews, but this guy came all the way out here and he seems real nice and—"

"No interviews."

"I know you're worried about it turning into a freak show and all, but—"

"No."

"All right. If you're going to be that way about it, I'll let him talk to one of the other magicians. He wanted you, though."

"I'm sure the other magicians give better interviews, anyway."

"I'll tell him that. Um, one last thing."

"What's that?"

"When do you think you'll be ready to, um, do an actual run-through? I mean, with the gun and everything?"

"Tomorrow at the dress rehearsal. I'll have it all ready

139

by then. Will that give you enough time to nail down all the lighting and blocking?"

"Sure thing," she said. "No problem. And, uh—good luck. I mean it. Really."

"Thanks," I said. "Mondo thanks."

I slipped out a side door just to make certain I didn't run into the reporter. It wasn't that I'm averse to publicity. Far from it. I just didn't want to have to explain myself in advance. One way or another, everything would become clear soon enough. If things went one way, I might wind up feeling a little foolish. I've lived with worse. But if they went another way, I'd be glad I had kept my mouth shut.

There was a phone booth on the corner, but the receiver had been ripped out. I found another one two blocks away, near a bus shelter that displayed a poster for the *Cavalcade* anniversary. The poster showed a large logo from the original show, the date, time, and channel of the reunion broadcast, and the words WILL LIGHTNING STRIKE TWICE? written across the top in bold, portentous type. Nobody had consulted me about the catchy headline. I didn't think much of it.

I got a little nervous when Clément didn't answer his phone right away. In light of recent events, it was easy to imagine he'd been sawed in half or beaten to death with a pack of cards or something. He finally picked up on the eleventh ring.

"Sorry," he said. "I was in the bathroom."

"No problem. Everything all right there?"

"I'm still alive, thank you very much."

"Did you manage to make that call?"

"It took some doing, but yes."

"And?"

A heavy sigh came through the earpiece. "Red Katz is still alive."

"Did you speak to him?"

"I found it most distasteful."

"But you did speak to him?"

**140**

"Yes. For the first time in decades. But he's not the man he once was. I believe he's not quite right in the head. He went nearly mad at the sound of my voice. His daughter says he's becoming more difficult every day. He lives with her now, out in Passaic."

"What's the address?"

"It won't do you any good to go out there. Katz was quite specific about that."

"But I have to talk to him! It's—"

"I didn't say he wouldn't talk to you. That's not the problem. In fact, he's quite eager to see you again. He was most interested in your career as a magician, although when I told him about the history studies you'd abandoned—"

"Edouard, can I see him or not?"

"Yes, but it has to be at a time and place of his choosing. He was very insistent on that. I think he believes he's still doing intelligence work."

"Did he say when and where?"

"Midnight tonight at Grant's Tomb. I believe the location was selected in deference to you."

I closed my eyes and leaned my head back. After a moment I said, "You're serious, aren't you?"

"He's serious. I told you he seemed a bit unstable."

"Am I supposed to wear a red carnation?"

"He said he would be able to recognize you from television."

"I'm gratified."

"Be careful with him, Paul. I don't know what it is you feel you need to know about that night—the night of the broadcast—but Katz is not a man to be taken lightly. Even now."

"Thanks. You be careful, too, Edouard. It might be a good idea to lay off the magic tricks for a couple of days."

After we said good-bye, I dialed my roommate at his office and asked if I could come by. If I'd had any brains, that would have been my last call. I thought about it for a moment, then I dropped in some more coins and dialed the number.

Clara hadn't spoken to me in two days, not since I'd told her I was going to do the bullet catch after all. Her last words to me had been unpleasant ones, about failure to grow up, excessive vanity, and irrational needs to demonstrate manhood. Then she'd gotten really tough.

Franklin answered the phone. "It's Paul, Franklin," I said. "How are you?"

"Okay," he said.

"What are you doing?" I asked.

"Watching cartoons," he said.

"Anything good?"

He mentioned the name of a program I'd never heard of and gave me a brief rundown of the plot.

"Is your mom around?" I asked.

"She said she didn't want to talk to you. Sorry."

"That's okay. She's still mad, huh?"

"Really mad. She says it's like you never growed up."

"Grew up," I said. "It's as if I never grew up."

"Grew up."

"Let me ask you something. Man to man. What would you do if you were me?"

"If my mom was mad at me, you mean?"

"Right."

"I'd go into my room and not come out for a while."

I told him that, for a variety of reasons, I felt like doing just that.

# Chapter 13

I hadn't seen H. Michael Clayton, my best friend and former roommate, since I'd gotten us tossed out of our apartment. Naturally I thought he might still be mad at me. So it gave me something of a start, when I knocked on the open door of his office, to see him standing there with a gun in his hands.

I suppose I shouldn't have been surprised. Michael usually had some form of ordnance around. Once I'd swept into the room to find myself staring down the barrel of a twelve-pounder Napoleon field cannon.

"Rifle musket?" I asked, by way of greeting.

"Fifty-eight caliber," he said, holding the piece up to the fluorescent ceiling light. "Nice, isn't it? Nine-pound muzzle loader. I know a guy out in Montana, this will just fill out his collection."

Unlike certain other people, Michael had gotten his doctorate in American history on time and with a minimum of fuss, although I don't think he'd ever intended to go into teaching. Within a year of graduation he'd set himself up as a one-man clearinghouse of Civil War documents, letters, uniforms, and weaponry. Whenever some cavalry colonel's battered old trunk turned up in an attic in South Carolina, Michael caught the next flight out. Whenever some elderly weapons buff decided to part with a few Spencer repeating carbines, Michael got a call. He has since established himself as a kind of collector's matchmaker, seeing to it that the owner of the cavalry colonel's trunk and the collector of cavalry medals find out about each other. The ten percent commission he earns on all successful transactions keeps him from having to work the family's tobacco business in Virginia.

It's difficult to imagine anyone better suited to the job. He even looks the part, with a pot-bellied shape, Vandyke beard, and small, round gun-metal glasses that give him the aspect of an unreconstructed Confederate officer.

I looked around the office for other new acquisitions. There were a few more Mathew Brady photographs on the walls, some new books piled on the floor, and some yellowed documents stacked on the desk. He'd also set up a cot in the corner.

"Listen," I said, gesturing toward the cot, "I spent some time on the phone with our good landlord this morning, establishing your alibi. I'm guessing you might be forgiven if you want to stay on in the apartment. He'll probably let you off with a minor rent hike."

"Not necessary. I have a bid in on a bigger place, nearer to here. Give me some room for my books. I'll be glad to be rid of you, anyway. You always left the cap off the toothpaste."

"You're not going to pump me full of lead, then?"

"Wouldn't that be redundant?" he asked, pleasantly enough. When I didn't respond, he turned his attention back to the rifle musket. "I got this from a guy in Atlanta. Did the deal over the phone. He didn't quite know what he had. I'm guessing it came from the Richmond armory, made with captured plates. Accurate up to six hundred yards. Real sniper's rifle. This could be the model that killed your pal General Sedgwick. Here, take a look."

"No thanks," I said.

Michael set down the gun and gave me an appraising stare as though I'd confirmed some long-held suspicion. Then he took off his glasses and began polishing the lenses on his tie, something he always did to help bring himself into the present century. "You know, Paul," he began quietly, "when I heard that you were going to do this television thing—I had to read about it in the paper, incidentally— I found myself in a real quandary. Why, this couldn't be my old chum Paul they're talking about, I told myself. My old chum Paul has a bona fide aversion to firearms. Never seen him touch one. He *knows* about them, certainly. But he never touches them." Michael put his glasses back on. "And then I got a message down in Virginia: Not only is Paul going to step in front of a loaded gun, but he wants *me* to furnish the gun. I tell you, I felt snafflehooped."

"Excuse me?"

"Snafflehooped. It's something we used to say back home. Means turned inside out."

I unfolded a canvas camp chair and sat down. "The gun has to be the same model my father used. I thought with your contacts you could get it for me in a hurry and at the best price."

Michael started shaking his head, presumably over my curious northern ways. He stepped behind his small missionary desk and picked up a long object wrapped in oilcloth. "It wasn't easy to find," he said. "A .557 Nitro Express. Just like Dad's. There's a strap and a night scope back there too. You might as well take them with you. You're paying an arm and a leg for them. What are you making on this TV show, anyway?"

I named a figure.

"The gun's costing you almost twice that. And I'm afraid I'm going to have to charge my normal commission on top of that. I know you wouldn't want me to put an insulting discount on my services." He unwrapped the cloth and let it drop to the floor, cradling the gun in both arms. "This one is a real beauty, Paul," he said, fingering

**145**

the long barrel. "Look at the rosewood. Any idea why your father picked it for his act?"

"The size, probably. He must have figured that even the people in the back rows would be impressed."

"Mind if I ask what happened to the original?"

"My mother had it destroyed a week or so after the funeral."

"Mind if I ask—"

"It's personal, Mike. I really don't want to go into my reasons."

He did some more head shaking. "So you said on the phone. You made that very clear. Well and good. So. The gun's in perfect working order. I had a mechanic check it over, and I took it out to the range myself this morning. Fired all ten rounds I got from the dealer. It has a hell of a kick. I've got some more shells on order; I'll have to drop them over to you later."

"It only has to fire twice. Once in dress rehearsal and once for the broadcast. After that I'll never do this trick again."

"I'd like to believe that, pal. I really would. But suppose someone calls up and offers you ten grand to do it out in Vegas? 'Just one more time,' you'll say. 'Then I'll hang it up.' Or what if you get more TV offers? I can see it now. You'll be the sidekick of some television detective, right? During the gun battles you'll leap out and catch the slugs in your teeth."

"I think you've made your point."

"Have I? Paul, this is an elephant gun. This gun could take you apart. I don't know what demon has possessed you, but I'd sure as hell like to know how you intend to survive—"

"Mike, I—"

"Relax. In seven years you never told me how the rabbit gets in the top hat, so I don't expect you to give away any secrets now. I figure you'll switch bullets, rig the chamber, something like that. That's not what's really bothering me."

I fixed my eyes on an unframed photograph of A. P. Hill tacked up over the desk. I didn't ask Michael what was really bothering him.

"What's really bothering me," he said after a while, "is that a trick like this is dangerous, even if you know what you're doing. Guns are dangerous. Always."

"I've been hearing that around."

"Even if the magic-trick part of it is foolproof, and even if you manage to account for the hundreds of things that can go wrong with a loaded firearm, it's still a damn fool thing to do. I hate to sound like a mother hen, but I just don't approve. You know I'm no gun-control fanatic. Hell, Paul, I never told you this before, I always figured it would upset you, but the entire time we lived together I kept a loaded forty-five automatic in the drawer of my nightstand. A Colt Commander."

"To pick off the cockroaches?"

"So that if anyone ever broke in and threatened my life, I could blow his head off. I guess that's my point, Paul. I know that guns exist and I know what they're for. I'm a military historian, for God's sake. Cold Harbor, Verdun, the Bulge—I know what happened there. A lot of people half my age got their insides spilled on the ground. There's nothing glamorous about it. That's my problem here. I know what you're doing is only a magic trick, but it sets a dangerous example. It promotes the comic book view of violence, that guns are somehow manly and dramatic and that nobody really gets hurt as long as the hero has the proper glint in his eye. I mean, the whole appeal of this trick you're doing is wrapped up in whether or not you die. I think it's twisted."

I drew in my breath and held it for a moment. "I agree," I said.

Michael started going through his desk drawers. I knew he was looking for one of his smelly black cheroots. "Somehow, my friend, that rings a little hollow."

"I mean it. You know that thing in the kitchen I use to chop vegetables?"

**147**

"The guillotine thing?"

"Right. Did you ever wonder where that came from? It used to be a magic trick. When I put together my first act, I paid a lot of money for that. It's called a wrist chopper. You'd put a carrot or a stalk of celery in the small top and bottom holes, and a volunteer's wrist between them in the larger center hole. The trick, obviously, was to slice through the vegetables without separating the volunteer from his hand."

Michael grunted and pushed his desk drawers shut, having failed to find his cigars. "That sounds a little Gothic," he said.

"Trust me—there was no hint of danger. You could saw away on a person's wrist all day with the thing and never even break the skin, but obviously the drama of the effect depends on the audience believing that someone could lose a hand."

"What fun."

"Believe it or not, a lot of magicians make a pretty funny routine out of it. They empty out a basket full of plastic severed hands, crack jokes along the lines of 'Let's give this brave soul a hand, he'll need it.' You get the idea. The first time I did it—bear in mind I was about fifteen years old—I called up this eight-year-old girl in a maroon velvet dress. Big cow eyes, brown hair with blue barrettes. She'd been hanging back all day, too timid to play any of the games or talk to the other kids. A lot of kids are afraid of magicians and clowns."

"Possibly they're afraid of getting their hands chopped off."

"Possibly. So I brought her to the front of the room, set up the guillotine, and let fly with the wacky patter, and when I took her hand to put it under the blade, she was shaking so much I couldn't go through with it. I pressed a piece of candy into her hand and sent her back to her seat. As epiphanies go, it was a minor one. But I'd arrived at an important decision about what was magic and what wasn't. I never did another trick that depended on fear or potential violence for its effect. I never even sawed a lady in half."

"So what you're saying is, 'Thanks very much for your concern, Mike, but keep out of it,' right?"

"I mean it in the nicest possible way."

"And it's all got something to do with these old men you were telling me about?"

"It's more than that now."

"I looked into that, by the way. All that stuff you were telling me about Katzenbacher's circus."

"And?"

He gave a shrug. "It's pretty much as I expected. Maybe it happened, maybe not. There's no way of confirming it. Your friend Clément didn't share too many details, and he put a nice gloss on what he did say. But I found instances of similar things happening, so who can say? That's the thing about history, Paul, and you should keep it in mind tomorrow night."

"What's that?"

"It has a way of repeating itself."

# Chapter 14

I decided to spring for a cab back to the pastry shop, figuring it might attract some unwanted attention if I carried a rifle onto the subway. I had several hours to kill before my midnight meeting at Grant's Tomb with Red Katz. I had two choices. I could stare at the walls of my new apartment, or I could pull a shift at Hugo's. My heart wasn't really in either option, so I decided to go for the paying one.

I changed my shirt and put on yet another of my four ties, this one a blue wool knit with festive gray horizontal stripes. Then I went about the business of preparing for an evening's close-up work. First I trimmed my fingernails and snipped off a potentially troublesome hangnail. Next I loaded up my pockets with small effects—a paddle trick, a himber wallet, and a couple of locking coin sets—and clipped some extra coins behind my lapels and some extra cards under the skirt of my jacket. Finally I packed my small briefcase with twelve decks of cards, a fifty-foot hank of rope, a pair of scissors, and a dice-stacking cup. I left for Hugo's just after six.

I decided to walk down Amsterdam to the bar. On the way I thought about Red Katz. The last time I'd seen him, I decided, he'd been giving me horsey rides in the front hallway of my parents' apartment on East Fifty-seventh Street. The next time I'd see him it would be midnight at a graffiti-scarred mausoleum near Harlem. I tried to sort through all the reasons why I couldn't just hop a bus to Passaic, meet his daughter, and have a nice cup of tea while Red and I talked about old times. I decided that Red Katz was very dangerous or completely crazy. Either way, I figured I'd need some company.

Giunt was working his usual corner at Broadway and Seventy-third, crouched low behind an upturned cardboard carton that had once held a microwave oven. Before him on the makeshift table were three playing cards, face-down and creased lengthwise like three tiny pup tents. Giunt wore his usual work clothes: a blue hooded sweatshirt zipped up over a white shirt, the tails of which hung down over a pair of shiny brown polyester slacks. The hood of Giunt's sweatshirt was pulled up tight around his face, almost covering his close-set brown eyes and his tight, flat line of a mouth. As usual, he had a pretty good crowd going.

Four years earlier, in a fit of public-spiritedness, I had signed up as a Big Brother. I had visions of myself and some bright-eyed city kid going to baseball games and playing Frisbee in the park. Instead I got Giunt. The endeavor was not a great success. Already a hard case at thirteen, Giunt stuck with me just long enough to satisfy his Youth Services case worker. In that time he got me to teach him enough magic to run a profitable street con.

You've probably seen the three-card monte. You'll be walking along Broadway or Lexington and you'll notice a big crowd of people gathered around some scruffy-looking street punk. Maybe you've got some time to kill, so you work your way closer, thinking that no harm can come to you with all these people around. Before you know it you're captivated by the unexpected grace of this kid in the hooded zip-front sweatshirt. It's amazing, really, the way he's got those cards dancing on that wobbly cardboard box.

The object of the game is obvious: keep track of the black card, the ace of spades. There are only three cards, the ace and two red queens, but the kid keeps lifting them, showing the faces and throwing them down again in a rapid-fire figure-eight pattern, so it's hard to keep track. It's like the old shell-and-pea game, only with cards. You're sure there's some trick to it, but still it doesn't seem so tough to spot the ace. A man in a Burberry raincoat throws down a twenty, and sure enough, he comes up a winner. Hell, you think, I can do that. I spotted that one too. Before you know it, you're reaching for your wallet. You can afford twenty bucks. A minute later you're mad at yourself because you got it wrong. You almost bet on the one at the end, but you changed your mind at the last minute. You reach for your wallet again. You'll get it this time.

At this point you might want to consider folding up your money and slipping it down the nearest sewer grating. It amounts to the same thing.

I could see about two hundred dollars in the hands of the players crowded around Giunt's microwave carton. I stood and watched for a few minutes. He was using red bicycle backs. I fiddled around in my pocket for a minute, then edged forward through the crowd, jostling the carton with my foot.

"Watch it, friend," Giunt said without looking up.

"Excuse me," I said. "Profoundest apologies, I am sure. Are you available Thursday next?"

Giunt's face darkened as he recognized my voice. He looked up from the cards, narrowing his brown eyes as if willing me to go away.

"I'm just on my way to a club meeting, you see, and it strikes me that your little amusement concession here might be of some interest to the fellows there."

Giunt scowled and began to throw the cards.

"We're having our annual 'Evening in Monte Carlo,'" I continued. "It promises to be quite a gala affair. We'd pay for your time, of course."

"Friend, you might want to think about moving aside." Giunt tried to make his voice as menacing as possible without scaring off any customers.

"You must understand, of course, that the lads down at the lodge are of a cautious and, I dare say, frugal disposition. They would demand some assurance that the gaming would be fair."

In the crowd I saw three of Giunt's shills—including one I hadn't spotted—move forward. Giunt shook his head. "Perhaps the gentleman would like to make a bet or move aside?" he said.

"I'm afraid I'd only be taking advantage of you. Down at the firm I am acquiring a reputation as something of a gambler. Just three weeks ago I cleared nine dollars in the football pool." I leaned forward conspiratorially. "I have a system, you know."

"Look, friend," said Giunt, biting down hard on each word, "I'm not interested in any—"

"Would you have any objection to dressing the part of a casino dealer? Do you, in fact, own a tuxedo? We would, of course, provide the leopardskin fez—"

I felt a strong hand grip my arm from behind. I quickly held up fifty dollars. "Shall I make a wager?" I asked. My arm was released.

"You're going to play?" Giunt asked, clearly relishing the prospect.

"Certainly," I said.

Giunt grinned and began throwing the cards again. He'd gotten better since I'd seen him last. His arms moved like two interlocking windmills.

"Pardon me," I said. "I'm sorry to be such a bother, but I wouldn't think of chancing my money without first examining those three cards."

"Friend—"

"It's not that I don't trust you, of course, it's just that my friends down at the lodge would insist—"

"I'm telling you, friend—"

I turned to a guy I'd seen lose on the previous throw. "Don't you think I should be allowed to examine the cards, sir?" I asked.

"Well, yeah," he said. "I guess so. Sure."

"What about you," I said to another recent loser. "Don't you think I ought to be allowed to examine them?"

"Absolutely," he said.

I looked down at Giunt. Grunting, he gathered up the three cards and handed them to me. I crouched down over the carton. "Now then," I said, "how do you throw them down? Like this?" I made a few awkward tosses, crudely imitating Giunt's fluid figure eight.

"Just like that, friend. See? Now give me the cards back."

"The ace is here, the two queens here. I throw them down . . . gee . . . not as smoothly as you did, I'm afraid. Now I turn them over . . . this is odd! Now there are two aces and one queen! How did that happen? Let's try it again."

"Friend, you'd better—"

"I throw the cards down again . . . how very peculiar! Now all three cards are aces!"

I started to gather up the cards for another throw, but the damage had been done. All that was left of Giunt's crowd were his three shills. They didn't seem to see much humor in the situation. Their spirits brightened a little when I set my fifty dollars down on the cardboard carton.

Giunt's two lookouts drifted over from where they'd been keeping an eye out for police. "You want us to kill him?" One of them asked.

"In a minute. You got something you want to say to me, Paul?"

"That job I got you at Tannen's didn't pan out, I see."

"It sure didn't. Thanks for nothing, buddy. They wanted a stock boy, not a counterman."

"Everyone has to start somewhere."

"Hey Paul? You come all the way here to tell me that?"

"I need a favor."

"A favor. I love this. I can't wait to hear what it is."

"I need a big brother."

"Protection?"

"More like a friendly neighbor."

Giunt narrowed his eyes again. It made for an impressively threatening expression.

"I'll pay," I said. I scooped up a bent card from the cardboard carton and snapped my finger against it. "And I'll show you how to keep nosy magicians out of your hair."

"Only one I'm worried about," Giunt said.


I did well in tips that night at Hugo's. People flocked in to see the guy who was going to get shot at on TV the following evening. Most nights I'll spend a fair amount of time table-hopping, but that night I never got out from behind the bar. In between tricks I deflected questions and listened to witty customers advise me against making long-term investments.

Strangely enough, I was on a hot streak all night. The cards did whatever I wanted, even when I got ambitious and tried some rigorous Ted Annemann routines. My centerpiece—a flashy, penetrating silver-dollars effect—actually had the crowd gasping.

Under normal circumstances I'd have worked until one or two in the morning, pushing myself with harder and fancier tricks until I started to make mistakes. Then I'd have let the house buy me a drink and congratulated myself on what a great night I'd had. That's what I'd have liked to do. Instead I knocked off shortly after eleven and took the M104 bus uptown to keep my midnight rendezvous.

I got off the bus at 116th Street and cut across the Barnard campus to Claremont and then Riverside Drive. I turned north on Riverside, walking quickly and trying to look purposeful.

As soon as Grant's Tomb was in sight, I started looking around for the backups Giunt had promised. Near a Dumpster on 122nd Street I spotted a rusted old Cougar that might have been friendly, but I couldn't tell for sure. As I crossed Riverside, another junker, a Dart, flashed its lights. I kept walking. I can't say I felt reassured exactly.

Ulysses Simpson Grant has never been my favorite Civil War general. He's not even in my top ten. The store clerk from Galena, Illinois, who rose to become Lieutenant General of the Union Army has always seemed to me a grossly overpraised figure. Although his drinking problem wasn't as bad as popular lore would have one believe, his generalship wasn't nearly as good. Say what you will about Grant's quiet resolve in the face of death and his gritty determination to do what needed to be done, but I've always had a sneaking preference for Sherman.

That's actually what I was thinking about as I climbed the granite steps and passed through the stone columns of the mausoleum. I remembered why I'd come when I saw that the bronze doors of the vault were ajar. I took a good look at the locks on the doors on my way in. I was impressed that Katz had gotten past them.

It was pitch-black inside the tomb, and I stood in the doorway for a moment trying to let my eyes adjust. I knew from previous visits that the main interior floor was built around a circular cutout that looked down to the sunken crypt where the twin sarcophagi of Grant and his wife lay. I also knew that if I didn't watch my step, I could topple over the railing and fall to the lower level.

I hadn't thought to bring a flashlight, but I had a production candle with me from my shift at the bar. I pulled the candle from my pocket—already lit, that's the effect—but its feeble flame did little to dispel the darkness.

I decided to make a little noise. "Katz?" I called. My voice echoed off the marble walls. I advanced a few steps into the tomb.

"Katz? Are you in here? Ho-Ho? Feel like giving me a horsey ride?"

Finally I saw him, sitting on a stone bench. He'd looked better. The bright red hair had thinned out, leaving only a few dirty orange tufts. The skin was pasty and the jowls were long and saggy. Also, there was a bruise under his left eye and an arrow imbedded in his forehead.

I dropped my production candle, and when I stooped down to pick it up, it took several minutes before the dizziness subsided enough for me to stand up again. When my head cleared, I found myself standing at the railing and looking down into General Grant's crypt. I was beginning to muster some respect for the general's quiet resolve in the presence of death.

# Chapter 15

The brown water stain over Lieutenant Chasfield's desk had grown larger in my five-day absence. The spreading mark no longer resembled Ohio. Probably there was a leaky pipe up there somewhere. I thought of pointing this out to the lieutenant, but he didn't seem much in the mood. Besides, the image of him being drenched in a sudden shower of dirty water and acoustical tile wasn't altogether unpleasant.

It was two in the morning and Chasfield had obviously been roused from sleep. Evidently a deep sleep. His hair was still mussed, his eyes were red, and he had the look of a man who had dressed in the dark. He almost dropped the thick manila file folder handed to him by the desk sergeant, and he seemed to have trouble understanding what was being said to him by a shortish man with a camera. Then my lawyer, Eileen Hopper, said a few choice things to him, and after that he looked even more mussed up.

I'd watched all this through the glass partition that separated the squad room from Chasfield's office, where

I'd been luxuriating in one of his metal folding chairs. The lieutenant didn't even look at me when he finally made his way into the office. Instead, he set down the manila folder, opened a desk drawer, pulled out a small glass carafe, and left the office with it. When he came back a minute later, the carafe was full of water. Chasfield went into another drawer and brought out two Styrofoam cups, a coil heating element, and a jar of instant coffee.

"That's a hell of a lawyer you got there, kid," Chasfield said at last.

"Oh?"

"A hell of a lawyer. She threw a good scare into Sergeant Richman. Moistened his zipper a little."

"Maybe she's a little peeved. Usually the most I ask of her is to look over my television contracts. I almost never get her out of bed at one in the morning because I'm being held on murder charges."

Chasfield lowered the heating coil into the carafe and plugged the cord in behind the desk. Then he carefully spooned some coffee into the cups. "No formal charges were made," he said. "Richman told her that. There was no reason to drag me down here. This all could have waited until morning."

"Eileen seemed to think it was either your beauty sleep or me spending the night in a holding cell. It wasn't a hard choice."

Chasfield gave a hollow laugh, as if trying to establish that he could be a sport. The water in the carafe started boiling. He mixed up two cups of instant coffee and handed me one. "You know what a crossbolt is?" he asked, swinging his feet onto the desk. "A crossbolt is a short arrow, about six inches long. More like a long dart, really. Anyway, that's what we found in your friend Katz's skull. I saw it myself. Stopped off on the way down here."

"Sorry to have missed you," I said.

"Are you now." Without taking his feet off the desk,

Chasfield reached for the folder and transferred it to his lap. "My boys were a little puzzled," he said, paging through the file. "They couldn't figure out what could fire a small arrow like that with enough velocity to enter the man's skull like it did. Seems a regular bow is too big, and a smaller one wouldn't have the necessary twang. Then somebody gets the bright idea to give Dr. Yumaki a call."

"Yumaki?"

"Retired ballistics guy. Forty-two years. Real expert. So we wake up old Yumaki, describe the arrow sticking out of your buddy's skull, and sure enough he rattles off the answer. 'Pistol crossbow,' he says." Chasfield looked up from the folder. "You know what that is?"

I shook my head.

Chasfield pushed a sketch across the desk. It showed what looked like a horseshoe mounted vertically on a pistol grip. "Dr. Yumaki says that's probably our murder weapon," Chasfield said. "Trouble is, these things are supposed to be real rare. Almost impossible to find. Even Yumaki's never seen one. So there's not much chance of finding it registered down at the license bureau, and I'm not sure where to begin looking for it, except by asking the guy who happened to be there standing over the body."

"I prefer to be known as the guy who called it in."

Chasfield smiled. It was actually kind of a nice smile. "The guy who calls it in is often the guy who did it, kid."

I returned my attention to the ceiling. "Shouldn't I have my lawyer in here for this?" I asked. "I mean, since she came all the way down here and all?"

"Relax. This is a private chat with your neighborhood cop. You make a lousy murder suspect. Seems Katz had been dead for more than an hour before you even got there. Those friends of yours? In the cars outside? Not the best eyewitnesses, I hear, but good enough. They saw you go in right at midnight. Katz was already dead by then, and your alibi for the time of death is pretty good."

"I don't suppose the guys outside saw anybody else go in or out?"

Chasfield shook his head as he slipped on his horn-rimmed bifocals. "It was probably over before they got there," he said. "So that just leaves you. Everybody's favorite Mr. Wizard. The guy who seems to be on hand for all the really colorful murders in this city. 'Course I could still nail you for trespassing, maybe a little B and E. Who knows, I might even get creative and dig up some kind of charge on defiling a national monument. Depends on how I feel after we have our little talk, uh?"

"I've already been through the whole story. Five times."

"Humor me. Humor an old man. What were you doing at the tomb?"

"I wanted to see who was buried there."

He took a sip of coffee. I'd already tried mine. It was terrible. "You know, now that I'm down here," he said, "I really don't care how long this takes."

There was nothing else to do but start at the beginning and repeat the whole story, with particular emphasis on what Clément had told me after Jacob Nussbaum's death. Chasfield was a good listener. He kept a poker face while I gave the details of Katzenbacher's circus, and he tried to look earnest when I moved on to the black market, but his composure cracked when the West German government got involved. "That's just a bit rich," he said. "Even for you."

"I'm just telling you what Clément told me," I said.

"Is that why you wanted to see Katz? Confirmation? I know I'd like some."

"Not exactly. I had to find out something about what happened later. That night in 'fifty-nine. Katz was the one, you know, who—"

"I know. I remember. He was the guy who got worked over that night."

I nodded and took another swallow of instant coffee. "I think it's pretty obvious that Katz knew more than he ever let on about that whole thing. I think he had something he wanted to tell me. I made it clear to Clément that that's what I wanted to talk to him about."

"You never talked to Katz directly?"

"Not directly, no."

"Why the midnight meeting? Why Grant's Tomb? You think maybe he was losing his grip?"

"I think he was scared. He had reason enough to be after Schneider and Nussbaum both got killed. Maybe Katz got one of those broken wands too."

Chasfield took off his glasses and rubbed at his red, hairy nose. "The broken wands," he said. "I love that detail. It's so *real*. Tell me something, did Clément set up the whole deal? The meeting with Katz?"

"That's right."

"Can you think of any reason why Clément might want to get rid of Katz?"

"Nope."

"Think real hard."

"If I were an inventive sort, I could probably come up with several reasons. But what's the point? He's not capable of it. I've known him all my life. He gave me my first Svengali deck."

"But up until three days ago you didn't know a thing about any of this Resistance stuff."

"It's not the same thing."

"No? You can't have it both ways, kid. If the Resistance story is true, then you have to believe he's capable of murder. What do you think they'd do, tie up enemy soldiers and leave little notes pinned to their chests? If he was in it for any length of time, he did some killing, let me tell you. And it's not such a hard knack to remember." He ran his fingers through his thin brown hair. "Besides, I forgot to share one other fact with you. Something else I got from Dr. Yumaki. It seems these pistol crossbows were developed during World War Two for the Office of Special Services."

I thought about that for a minute. "That's very interesting," I concluded.

"Isn't it, though."

"Clément never claimed to be OSS, though. Besides, what's his motive?"

"I don't know. It's just funny how he's the only one of that bunch left alive. You say he's a cripple?"

"No. He just has arthritis in his hands."

"So maybe he's crazy jealous of those other guys who can still do magic—you know, the ones who were going to be on that television special."

"That seems a little implausible."

I regretted it as soon as I said it. Chasfield threw back his head and gave a long, hoarse laugh that resolved itself in a coughing fit. "Honest, Lieutenant Chasfield, sir," he said when he had caught his breath, "they were all Resistance heroes! Don't you believe me?" He swung his feet to the floor and slapped the folder down on the desk. "Got to be honest with you, kid. I like to deal with good old-fashioned killings. You know, jealous husbands, crimes of passion, that kind of stuff. These cute little magic murders leave me cold. So does this Resistance yarn. Implausible? This whole thing strikes me as paper thin. Not to mention unverifiable. And whose word do we have for it? That's the part I really like. Who's bringing us all these interesting stories? Your friend Clément, that's who."

"I still believe him," I said.

"That helps me a lot. Thank you." He took another sip of coffee.

"Suppose he did kill Katz. You think he also killed Nussbaum and Schneider?"

"So far I have only your say-so that their deaths were

murders at all. There's no proof. Not a shred. Sometimes a heart attack is just a heart attack, you know?"

"How about Nussbaum? Did he just spontaneously combust?"

"You're the one who told us there was usually a flash of fire in that trick. Maybe he just got careless. Or nervous. Maybe he just used too much of the—the stuff. What was it? Magnesium?"

"Right. Magnesium."

"Maybe he was trying to impress that hotshot director with a big bang. Who knows?"

"Couldn't happen. I know what I'm talking about here. That's what makes Katz's death different from the other two. Somebody spent a lot of time rigging up Schneider and Nussbaum's deaths. If I hadn't used those balloons of Schneider's, there'd be no reason to think there was anything unnatural about his heart attack. And if I weren't so familiar with Nussbaum's dove act, then I'd have to agree that maybe he'd somehow gotten careless. But Katz's death is totally different. When was the last time anybody got accidentally bored through the head with an arrow?"

Chasfield's smile had just the right touch of pity. "Excuse me. I forgot I was dealing with a gifted amateur. So, tell me, who aced Katz and why?"

"Take your pick of reasons. Maybe he was going to tell me something important about the other two killings."

Chasfield just rubbed his forehead.

"Have you got any better theories?" I asked.

"You sure you didn't do it?"

"Not that I can recall."

"A couple of guys out there tonight think Katz was just one of those dozens of people each year who take a trip to the wrong part of town at the wrong part of the night."

"Good thinking, Lieutenant. This was just another of those hundreds of pistol-crossbow killings you're always hearing about. It's just a lucky chance he wasn't boiled in oil."

"We get stranger things happening all the time, kid. Last month we had somebody skinned alive in Riverside Park. Just about anything your average freak or weirdo can think of, we've seen it. Twice."

"Even people getting shot to death on live television?"

Chasfield got up slowly from his chair and stared through the glass partition into the squad room. "You've got some half-cocked idea that all this has something to do with that night," he said.

"Another magician, another death."

"Is that why you want me along for the ride?"

"There's a certain appealing symmetry to it."

He turned to face me, leaning his back against the glass. "Kid, you know how badly that screwed up my life? I knew the minute I squeezed that trigger my life would never be the same. I just knew it. It's one thing to shoot a man in the line of duty. It's another thing to gun down a guy in a little top hat in front of the whole world. How do you think I felt, going to that funeral? The look on your mother's face when I tried to say something? Shit, the look on *your* face, that was something to see." Chasfield pushed off from the glass wall and turned to look back out into the squad room. "And then, when the shock of it all wore off and things started to get back into the routine, I had a new set of problems. I mean, what happened was tragic, sure. But it was also kind of ridiculous. Guys started making jokes. If I drew a parade detail, like, they'd say, 'Hey, Chasfield, don't shoot the clown!' Like that. I was never able to shake it off. Made things rough for me all down the line. May have been what kept me from making captain. That's what I tell my wife, anyway." He turned away from the glass wall and lowered himself into his desk chair. "So you think I feel like dredging it all up again? No thanks."

"Why don't you look at it as a chance for redemption of a sort?"

**166**

"That doesn't quite cut it," he said.

"Then why don't I talk to the producers and get them to give you a whole lot of money?"

A big smile spread across his face. "That would help," he said.

# Chapter 16

My lawyer and I parted company on the steps of the police station, after I had managed to convince her that, no, I really didn't want a ride home. She offered up some persuasive arguments about the lateness of the hour and the dubious nature of the neighborhood, but I held the day. I knew I'd have trouble sleeping that night, and I hoped the walk would wear me out. It seemed unlikely I'd stumble across any more dead bodies.

A cold, clear blackness pressed down on the streets as I headed home, making the lights from the all-night groceries and diners seem unnaturally bright. I passed a number of people on the street and none of us seemed in a particular hurry to get where we were going.

I made it back to Frieda's at about four in the morning. I felt tired, but I still didn't hold out much hope for sleep. I went around to the shop's kitchen-service entrance this time and wound up tripping the alarm, but I managed to shut it down in the allotted thirty seconds before the police relay went off. The noise rattled me, though, and I made my way across the kitchen and up the steps to my apartment like a man nursing a hangover.

Moonlight spilled in through the high windows, so I didn't switch on any lights in the apartment. I emptied my pockets of all the close-up apparatus and hung my coat in the Zigzag Lady cabinet. Then I loosened my tie and poured some food pellets into my rabbit's dish. "How do you like the new place?" I asked him.

"It's nice," said a voice.

If I'd had more energy, I'd have probably jumped out of my skin. As it was, I just turned slowly on my heel to see where the voice had come from. Clara was sitting across the room in what had once been part of a "Vanishing Swami Sedan Chair" illusion. She was awake, but barely.

"You make a lot of noise when you come in late, you know that?"

"You mean the alarm? Sorry. I didn't know anyone was in here. Pardon me all to hell."

"What time is it?"

"Four. Is there some kind of rooftop entrance to this place that I don't know about? How did you get in here?"

"Frieda let me in. I've been here—my God—for five hours. Where've you been?"

I spent a few minutes telling her.

"My night was almost as exciting," she said when I'd finished. "I helped Franklin with his coloring book. Then I watched a movie."

"Sounds great. Preferable, certainly." I clicked on the light bulbs that outlined the mirror of Schneider's dressing table. "I thought you weren't talking to me," I said, dropping my keys and wallet onto the table. "I thought I was in the doghouse."

"You are," she said without much conviction. "I came over here to make one last impassioned plea for you not to do the trick. I was going to convince you by whatever means necessary."

"The mind boggles."

"But that was five hours ago," she continued. "And since then I've done a lot of thinking. There's nothing more I can say. You've clearly made up your mind. The

**170**

thing that worries me, though, is that whatever's behind all this is obviously tearing at your insides. I mean, look at you. You look so rigid. So serious."

"Not long ago that was the whole problem with me. Not serious enough, someone said."

She gave a little snort from across the room. "When you first started poking around in this thing, you were getting some kind of a charge out of it. Oh sure, you were mourning your beloved mentor, but there was a part of you that was just eating it up with a spoon. The excitement, uncovering the Resistance intrigue, explaining the finer points of magic to poor, doddering old Lieutenant Chasfield . . ."

"Lieutenant Chasfield never doddered a day in his life."

"You know what I mean. Now, I don't know. I watched you while you taped that Stain Begone commercial the day before yesterday. You were so grim."

I sighed and slipped off my shoes. "Stain removal is no joke," I said.

"Ever since we saw the kinescope, you've had an edge. I know how traumatic that must have been, but there have to be better ways of dealing with it than doing what you're doing."

I sat down at the dressing table. Clara was a long way off in the sedan chair. "I'll survive the bullet catch," I said. "Don't worry. I'll come out of it without a scratch. It's the rest of it that's left its mark. I guess it never occurred to me that I might not get out clean. Everything got screwed up the minute I came on the scene. Two more people have died. I certainly didn't figure on that. I guess I had an idea of myself tracking down the killer just in the nick of time. You know, like just before he poisoned the city's water supply."

"And then?"

"Then? Then I'd hand him over to the authorities and ride off on my horse. You want a drink?"

"What do you have?"

"Anything you want." I got up and walked to a small fringed side table and picked up a rose-colored glass decanter filled with liquid. "Behold the mystic spirit bottle. What's your pleasure? Vodka?" I poured some clear liquid into a small glass and carried it over to her. "No ice. Sorry."

"Suppose I'd said Scotch?"

I poured again, filling a second glass with amber liquid. "Dewar's," I said, taking a sip.

"Not bad. What if I'd wanted a grasshopper?"

"Then I'd have had to kill you," I said. I took my Scotch and sat on one of the few nonmagic pieces of furniture in the room, a club chair that Schneider had picked up from a hotel liquidation sale. Something poked into my back. "What's this?" I reached behind my back and pulled out a large paper bag.

"Frieda asked me to give you that. She said your old roommate dropped it by."

I unfolded the top of the bag and lifted out a cardboard box full of shells for the Nitro Express. Each shell was a good three inches long. Clara frowned when she saw them. There was something else in the bag. A small plastic figure of an elephant with a tag tied around its neck. The tag read: "Lest we forget."

I tossed the toy elephant to Clara. "What's this mean?" she asked, looking at the tag. "Forget what?"

"It's kind of a private joke. Something that happened a long time ago."

"Before you left school, you mean?"

"Not exactly. This happened in 1864."

"Ah. A Civil War story. But of course." She got up from the sedan chair and began taking down her hair, which had been up in a loose bun. The hair falling down around her face made for a pleasant scene in the moonlight. "I'm game," she said. "Tell me a Civil War story. I'd enjoy hearing someone else's troubles."

"It's about our old friend General Sedgwick."

"Uncle John."

"Right. Have you ever read anything about Spotsylvania?"

"I frequently lie awake nights reading about Spotsylvania."

"Don't joke. I often do."

"I know." She held up a copy of *Campaigning with Grant* by Horace Porter. "It was all I could find to read while I was waiting for you. It was either that or *Tarbell's Course in Magic*."

"That's not a bad book. It's a memoir. Porter was an aide-de-camp of Grant's."

"So I gathered. I'd still have preferred a magazine." She sat down on the edge of the bed, kicked off her shoes and stretched her long legs slowly. A more perceptive man might have aborted the Civil War story.

"Spotsylvania," said Galliard, the incurable romantic, "was not General Sedgwick's finest hour. His men had been forced to march all night in order to get into position ahead of Anderson's Confederates. Grant wanted to push toward Richmond, Lee kept getting in the way. Nobody counted on having to fight again so soon—they'd just come off the Wilderness—but when the two armies met at Spotsylvania, it became obvious that there was a battle brewing. My man Sedgwick—the affable bachelor, the solitaire player, the best-loved man in the Army of the Potomac—was in command of the Sixth Corps."

Clara lay back on the bed and stretched her arms out over her head, arching her back a little. It was kind of distracting. I took a sip of my drink. "Sedgwick had a history of exposing himself needlessly to enemy fire. He'd been wounded twice in previous battles, and once he'd been hit in the stomach by a spent ball."

"A what?"

"A shot with almost all of its momentum expended. It just hit him and bounced off. Most men would have taken that as a sign to be more careful. Not Sedgwick. He liked to be seen at the front lines, it was good for morale.

**173**

So before the battle, he made a point of seeing to the placement of his artillery. There were some Confederate sharpshooters sending random shots into the Union lines, so a lot of veterans were taking cover. Bear in mind, in those days rifle fire wasn't terribly accurate at long ranges. Sedgwick wouldn't have thought he was in any real danger, even though a major general makes a pretty tempting target. Unknown to Uncle John, though, these particular sharpshooters were using captured Union long arms with a greater effective range than any of the old familiar Confederate weapons. Sedgwick either didn't know or didn't fully appreciate this."

"That fool," Clara said. "That foolish, irresponsible madcap—"

"So the general is strolling around on the breastworks, and every few minutes there's the crack of a rifle and everybody dives for cover as a bullet whistles by. Everybody except Sedgwick. Some of his men start shouting something to the effect of 'Get your butt down, sir,' but does Sedgwick listen? No. He smiles a little smile and says, 'Don't be ridiculous, men. They couldn't hit an elephant at this distance.' "

"And that's when they shot him," Clara said.

"Not just yet. First a soldier standing only a few feet away falls down dead. Sedgwick, never one to take a hint, says again, 'They couldn't hit an elephant at this distance.' " I took another sip of my drink.

"And *that's* when they shot him," Clara said.

"Under the left eye. Some people say he never got the word 'distance' out the second time, which makes for an even better story, if you think about it."

"How sad. Your favorite general. I'm so sorry."

"That's okay. Thanks for your concern."

Clara lifted up the plastic elephant and danced it along the edge of the bed. "Well, that certainly places Michael's message in an interesting light. 'Lest we forget.' What do you suppose he meant by that?"

"You got me. It's a real puzzler."

Clara sat up slowly. Then she carefully set the elephant on the nightstand and stood up. "Paul, you're a very stupid man," she said with great conviction. "Very stupid, indeed. You don't have to prove anything. Not to me, not to the world, not to Schneider, not to your father. Don't die just to prove something."

I sat very still and didn't say anything.

Clara sighed. "I didn't think that would do any good," she said.

"Don't think I don't appreciate the sentiment."

She kept standing there. After a while I could see she was crying.

I made up my mind about something. I walked over and pulled the .557 Nitro Express out from underneath the bed. Then I picked up the box of shells Michael had brought.

Clara, pausing in the midst of blowing her nose, said, "This isn't going to be one of those murder-suicide things, is it?"

"Almost as bad," I said. "I'm about to violate my sacred magician's oath."

"Is there really a sacred magician's oath? I've always wondered."

"Not really. It just gives us an excuse not to tell our friends and loved ones all the secrets. Watch me carefully. Pay close attention. You see this bullet?"

"I see it."

"Note that it has two parts: a shell casing and a slug. The casing holds the gunpowder charge. The slug is the actual projectile. When the firing pin of the gun strikes the base of the shell casing, the gunpowder ignites and sends the bullet flying out at an alarming speed."

"You don't say."

I walked over to the packing-crate coffee table. "Step over here to my laboratory, if you would. I have some things here that might interest you. Suppose I were to take

**175**

this nail file and these pliers and loosen the collar of the shell casing. Just like that. I'd be able to lift the slug right out of there. Neat, huh? Here, you hold the slug. Now suppose I were to stuff a little dab of this paraffin into the shell casing? That would seal the gunpowder in there and keep it from spilling all over the place. It would also effectively create a blank cartridge." I held up the doctored casing for Clara's inspection.

"But you don't really expect to get away with that, do you? You think no one's going to notice that the tip of the bullet is missing?"

"Heck, I guess you're right. You'd better give the slug back. I guess I'll have to cancel the show . . . say! Wait a minute. If I were to fit the slug back into the shell casing like this, it would look like a normal bullet, right? And then if I crimp it with the pliers a little bit, no one will ever notice that the casing doesn't fit quite as snugly as it once did."

Clara stared at the reassembled bullet. "Wax or no, if you load that thing into a rifle, it'll fire."

I set the bullet carefully aside. "You've grasped the problem beautifully," I said. "But the demonstration isn't quite over."

"It's not?"

"Not quite. Imagine if you will the scene tomorrow night on the stage of the *Magic Cavalcade* anniversary show. Everyone is breathless with anticipation. Most nervous of all is Lieutenant Harvey Chasfield, NYPD. That's one of the reasons I specifically wanted him. Not just because he was the one who pulled the trigger on my father, but because I know he'll be shaking in his shoes. You could tell on the kinescope he had stage fright; imagine him tomorrow night."

"Anybody'd be nervous in those circumstances. Why is that so important?"

"Because I'm planning for him to make a mistake. A fumble, if you will." I turned my back to Clara and fiddled with the bullet for a minute. "Have you ever held a gun before?" I asked.

"When I was a girl. Visiting my uncle on his farm."

I turned and handed her the bullet. "Load the rifle, please."

Reluctantly, she picked up the Nitro Express and took the bullet from my cupped hand. The shell slipped from her fingers as she went to load it into the breech of the rifle.

"Oops," I said. "Wonder how that happened. Could it have something to do with the rubber stopper I've jammed into the rifle breech? Or could the machine oil I coated the bullet with have been a contributing factor?"

"Let me get this straight. You intentionally made the bullet slippery?"

"And blocked up the gun barrel."

"I don't see how that helps you." She bent down to pick up the cartridge. It slipped from her fingers again. "If Chasfield can't load the gun, the trick's over before it can even begin."

"This just introduces a necessary extra step into the action. After the nervous lieutenant drops the bullet, Paul the experienced stage performer will step forward to lend a helping hand. The audience will get the impression that I hadn't planned to touch the bullet, so it won't occur to them that I might be working some unseen magic. Enforced fumbling. You'd be amazed how many tricks work on this principle. Only the enlightened among us know that there are no accidents in this world."

"Clever. What's that thing for?"

"This? It's the point of a drawing compass. I'll ask Chasfield to scratch some identifying marks onto the shell before he loads the gun. A penknife would work just as well. Any sharp metal point."

"Let me try." I held the bullet steady on a small china plate while Clara made some shaky hatch marks on the shell casing and slug. "Like that?"

"Just like that. Next I'll hold the bullet up to the camera to show the markings, and then my butterfingered marksman friend will try to load the gun. Should he happen to drop the bullet, I'll lend a hand." I loaded and cocked the piece.

"Great. Terrific. So there really is a—"

She never finished the thought because I chose that moment to aim the rifle at the nearest window and squeeze the trigger. The blast scared the hell out of her and probably woke up half of Manhattan. All in all, it was a stupid thing to do. The recoil banged the hell out of my shoulder.

Clara kept her eyes closed for a full minute. By the time she opened them and pulled her hands away from her ears, she had it figured out.

"The window," she said.

I nodded.

"It's not broken."

I nodded again.

"Where is it?"

Slowly, I drew back my lips into a broad smile. The bullet was clenched between my teeth.

"Son of a bitch," she said. "Son of a bitch. You must have—you probably lifted out the tip of the bullet. The slug part. Because the shell thing—the collar—was loose, you lifted it right out while you were loading the gun."

I took the bullet from between my teeth. "That left only the shell casing and the powder charge in the rifle. No bullet."

Clara took a couple of minutes to collect herself. Another vodka helped. "Look, Paul," she said after she'd thought it over for a while, "I'm not much of an expert, but even I know that a blank can kill someone. Or at least burn them pretty badly."

"That's what the pane of glass is for at mid-stage. It'll catch most of the powder and wax."

"Won't the audience catch on when it doesn't break?"

"It will break. There's a little coiled steel spring arm in the base. It'll pop up and shatter the glass just as the gun goes off, if my friend Henry remembers to pull the cord backstage."

"You seem to have covered all the bases, but I—"

"Not quite. There's still one detail I can't account for. When I catch the bullet, it'll show the markings that Chasfield scratched onto it, but there won't be any of the rifling marks that normally occur when a bullet is fired from a gun. Other magicians have figured out ways to create or duplicate the marks, but it usually involves a complicated handoff to an assistant backstage. I'm just going on the assumption that no one will notice in the excitement of the moment. It bothers me a little, though."

"That seems the least of your problems, considering that the whole trick hinges on whether or not Chasfield drops the bullet. Isn't that kind of chancy?"

"Not really. The rubber stopper I've got jammed up there is placed so that a whole bullet won't fit in the gun. The shell will slide in only when the tip is removed."

"Still, suppose something goes wrong? What if Chasfield doesn't drop it, and you don't get to handle the bullet yourself?"

"Then I go to Plan B."

"What's that?"

"Run like hell."

I took Clara's glass and refilled it from the rose-colored decanter.

"Paul," she said, "you figured all this out from the kinescope?"

"Yes."

"Then you also figured out what went wrong."

It wasn't a question, so I didn't answer.

"Do you want to tell me about it?"

I shook my head.

"But you're going to go ahead and do the bullet catch anyway."

I put down my glass and walked toward her. She met me halfway.

"Whatever it is, it must be pretty horrible, then," she said.

"It's more horrible than I ever could have imagined."

# Chapter 17

Clara had already left by the time I woke up the next morning. I got out of bed and padded around the room for a few minutes before I saw the note she'd left on the dressing-table mirror. It was a nice note; she wished me luck on the broadcast and promised to convey my regards to Franklin. She made it clear, however, that this was one time she didn't want to stick around to say any good-byes.

When I got through reading the note, I noticed how cold the floor was under my bare feet. I didn't have any slippers. I had no intention of buying any slippers either. I told myself that I liked to live dangerously. I'm just one hell of an amusing guy in the morning.

I picked up my pocket watch off the dressing table and popped open the cover. I'd slept all of three hours and forty minutes, pushing my total for the week to about fifteen or sixteen hours. I had a look at myself in the mirror. My eyes were red and shadowed with dark circles. My face had a sallow tinge. My teeth still looked pretty good, though.

I pulled on a white shirt, khaki pants, and tennis shoes, and went downstairs to the shop just in time to catch the tail end of the morning coffee break. One of the waitresses quickly folded back the page of the tabloid she was reading, but not before the headline DEADLY DATE WITH A BULLET leapt out at me.

I poured myself a cup of coffee and sat alone reading a discarded copy of *The New York Times*. I didn't speak to anyone and no one spoke to me.

After two cups of coffee I went back upstairs and got cleaned up. I wasn't due at the studio until late afternoon, and I wanted to keep myself as busy as possible until then. First I prepared and double-checked my equipment. That took about half an hour. Then I walked across the street to pick up my tails from the dry cleaner. That ate up another fifteen minutes. When I got back, I read a book for twenty minutes. I couldn't seem to concentrate so I checked over my equipment again. That killed another half an hour. Then I sat in a chair for about three and a half hours, getting up only twice. Once to put my clothes in a garment bag, and once because I'd forgotten to pack my cuff links.

At about three-fifteen I hailed a cab and gave the address of the studio in Queens. When the driver asked about the long, thin object wrapped in oilcloth, I told him I was going fishing.

This time I didn't need my Society of American Magicians card to get past the studio guard. He recognized me. Hardly anybody from the *Cavalcade* crew was there yet, so I decided to take a look around. I carried my equipment into the main studio and set it down at the foot of the stage. Even though the building was little more than a large warehouse, the crew had done a nice job of getting the look and feel of a turn-of-the-century music hall. They'd even managed to make the house look good; the plastic seats gave the appearance of wood and velvet from a distance, and some artfully designed panels along the walls created the impression of a balcony and boxes. It would make for a good effect when the cameras panned the audience for reaction shots.

I climbed onto the stage and started checking out angles and pacing off distances, making sure nothing had changed too much since I'd walked through the routine the previous day. Someone had hit on the inspiration of opening the show with a dance number, so the set was cluttered with fountains and flashpots. Two of the obelisks that had been part of the original *Cavalcade* set now supported a banner reading MAGIC'S A-COMIN'!

The entire stage would have to be cleared for my segment. Forrester had given me some trouble about that, but I stood my ground. I wanted the stage as stark as possible. No winking sphinxes, no Manhattan skylines, no Bullet's A-Comin'! banners. Just me, Chasfield, the metal tripod for the glass, and the gun.

I spotted the metal tripod standing in the wings and went to check it over. I slid out the pane of glass and pulled on the cord that tripped the spring arm. The mechanism worked perfectly, so I replaced the glass.

By this time the stagehands and technicians had started to arrive, and I knew I was going to be in their way. I had only one last thing to check out, but I didn't want anyone to see me do it. I walked over to the stage right fly curtain and pretended to examine somebody's Floating Lady equipment. Then I stole a glance upward at the flies. Everything looked all right, but I couldn't be sure.

Mindy Kramer, the associate producer, caught me lurking in the wings. "Are you trying to steal the other guys' secrets?" she asked, pointing at the Floating Lady.

"Actually, yes," I said. "This one's always baffled me."

"I'll bet," she said, pulling at the straps of a blue nylon backpack she had over her shoulder. "I didn't expect to see you here so early. None of the other performers are here yet. Hey, Chip's not even here yet. I just came in to check out some lighting cues, make sure of some stuff. You, too, huh?"

"It pays to be conscientious."

"Right. Well, I'll see you for the full dress." She started to walk off toward the control booth. "Oh, listen," she said, turning back, "I tried to get you your own dressing room, but we're a little tight on space. I had to put you in with Magic Phillip. You mind?"

"The world's most highly paid magician," I said. "I don't mind at all."

"Well, I figured you two being the youngest and all, you'd probably get along. I didn't want to put anybody in with that Yen Soo Kim guy. I'm not even sure if he speaks English."

"I'm sure Magic Phillip and I will become fast friends."

"Great." She turned away again. "Oh, right, one more thing. I almost forgot, since there's so much going on." She unslung her backpack and began digging through it. "These telegrams came for you earlier today. The usual good-luck stuff, I guess. Also, a package. I figured I'd better give it to you before the show. Where did I put it? A bicycle messenger brought it over. Maybe I left it—oh, here."

She handed me a blue and white courier pack and watched as I unfastened the string and looked inside.

"Huh," she said. "That's kind of a weird thing to send somebody, isn't it?"

"I've sort of been expecting it," I said. "It's part of a set."

"Yeah? What is it, some kind of good luck thing for magicians? You know, like actors say 'Break a leg'?"

I slipped the broken wand into my pocket. "That's right," I said. "It's for luck."

# Chapter 18

**M**agic Phillip, the world's most highly paid magician, turned his chair toward me and held up two wooden hangers. On one was a purple nylon T-shirt covered with blue comets that had glittery contrails. On the other was a green nylon T-shirt covered with orange moons and red stars.

"Which one do you think I should wear for the broadcast?" he asked.

"I don't know," I said. "It's a tough call."

He turned back toward the dressing-room mirror. "I didn't like how this pink one looked on camera. People might, you know, wonder about me. I think I'll go with the green. What do you think?"

"I think the purple brings out your high coloring."

"Yeah?" He lifted up the hanger with the purple shirt. "Maybe."

I'd met Magic Phillip only half an hour before, but already we were on familiar terms. I called him Magic, and he called me Dude.

"How do you think it's going, Dude?" he asked. "The dress rehearsal, I mean? Did you like my effect?"

"You were great," I said.

"Thanks. Hey, you must be real nervous. I'm always real up when I come off stage, even in rehearsal. It's an incredible rush, know what I mean? But you must be nervous."

"A little," I said.

"I mean, me, I'm lucky to have been invited to appear on this thing. And to think they actually let me open the show." He shook his head at this stroke of good fortune. "Those other guys, Sanderson and Merlini, they were actually on the original, so of course you'd want them. And I can understand booking Yen Soo Kim, considering he's never been on American television before. And you, well . . ."

Actually, the producers would cheerfully have sold the rest of the performers into slavery for an appearance by Magic Phillip. At the age of twenty-seven he'd already starred in a successful Broadway musical, several cable specials, and numerous international tours. Sutton Forrester, in particular, had been more than willing to stretch the concept of the reunion broadcast to include him. "Fresh blood," he'd said. "A little pizzazz."

Magic Phillip knew all there was to know about pizzazz. His real name had been Phillip Oberstein, but he'd had it legally changed a few years earlier because, as he said at the time, "A name is an effect and an effect is an illusion."

A dancer by training and a magician by default, Magic Phillip had created a school of magic that owed more to Busby Berkeley than Blackstone and Kellar. His tricks tended to be big, brassy, and more or less incidental to the choreography. The effect he'd chosen to open the *Cavalsade* broadcast was typical of the genre: He planned to vanish a parking lot full of Rolls-Royces. For added flair a remote camera would capture the trick through the legs of a kick line of Las Vegas show girls. I suppose it was a good stunt, but one very much out of step with the tone of the original *Magic Cavalcade*. In fact, the staging relied on satellite feeds and steady cams that didn't exist in those days. Call me old-fashioned, but I'd have rather seen him do a good, honest card trick.

Our dressing room came equipped with a ten-inch color monitor so we could keep track of the progress of the dress rehearsal. Yen Soo Kim was on stage doing his famous "Silken Rhapsody." I sat back to watch. I'd read about the routine, but never actually seen it. It had supposedly been first performed in the fourteenth century, for a descendant of Genghis Khan at the palace in Hangchau. Yen Soo Kim staged his presentation against a backdrop of painted screens that suggested the original setting.

Moving with a precise and economical grace, the magician produced a large crystal bowl and poured in various colored liquids. Then, pushing back the sleeve of his flowing ceremonial gown, he reached into the liquid to produce a series of flaming torches followed by a seemingly endless cascade of colorful silk flags knotted together at the corners. Assistants stretched the chain of flags up the aisles and into the audience. The monitor carried no sound apart from the camera cues being called from the director's booth, but I guessed the magician had chosen a quiet piece of classical Chinese music to accompany the effect. He rarely spoke on stage, except through an interpreter.

The Silken Rhapsody routine climaxed as Yen Soo Kim poured the bowlful of liquid into a large paper cone. Then he broke open the cone to produce a pair of white owls. It was a nice touch; Houdini had used an eagle during World War One.

I turned to see how Magic Phillip had enjoyed the effect, but he hadn't been watching. I started to tell him about it when Mindy Kramer knocked on the open door of the dressing room. "Merlini's up next, Paul," she said. "You're on deck."

I stood up and straightened my bow tie one last time. Magic Phillip flashed me a thumbs-up. "Knock 'em dead," he told me.

Mindy led me down a narrow, heavily trafficked corridor that connected the dressing rooms and the stage. People got out of the way to let us pass. Some even stopped their conversations mid-sentence to have a look at me.

I tapped Mindy on the shoulder. "Hey, Jonesy," I said, "you think the governor'll come through at the last minute?"

"What?" she asked.

"Never mind," I said.

Lieutenant Chasfield waited in the wings, looking rather distinguished in his dress uniform. A makeup woman was patting at his face with a powder puff, taking particular pains to camouflage his nose. Chasfield kept swatting her hand away until finally she gave up.

"I'm going to watch from the booth," Mindy told me. "Break a leg. Or a wand, as you magicians say."

"Thanks." I watched her head away.

Henry, my stagehand friend, sidled up and whispered, "Everything is all set. Just like you said. You should bring the house down."

"The cord," I said. "Can you get at it?"

He winked and retreated down the corridor, leaving me and Chasfield standing by ourselves in the wings. Chasfield already had the Nitro Express in his hands. "Nervous?" he asked.

I nodded. "You?"

By way of reply he reached into his hip pocket for a leather-covered flask. "I didn't know there'd be an audience for the dress rehearsal," he said.

"It's supposed to get us in fighting trim," I said.

"Why the cameras?"

"The technical side needs rehearsal too. Also, they're making a tape, in case there are any glitches in the live broadcast."

Chasfield took a sip from his flask and offered it to me. I shook my head.

We had a nice side view of the stage, where Matthew Merlini was several minutes into his routine. He'd performed all of three times on the original program, but when the supply of original cast members began to dwindle, he'd been flown up from Florida at the last moment to stumble his way through a Floating Lady act.

"I can't see any wires," Chasfield said.

"He's not using any wires."

"Huh. I always thought they used wires."

The curtains closed as Merlini got a nice hand from the audience. The crew swarmed over the stage to remove the set. Sutton Forrester's voice came over the backstage speakers, amplified with plenty of bass for a godlike effect. "Nice job, everybody. We're back from commercial in two minutes. Only seven seconds off pace. Stay loose for the big finale. Cue the dancers."

Merlini, looking a little lost in the rush, hurried off stage. "Good luck, son," he said, grasping my hand. "I knew your father." He stood for a moment, and I could tell he was trying to think of something appropriate to say. He couldn't seem to come up with anything, so he just shook my hand again and hurried toward the dressing rooms.

Chasfield wiped his forehead with a handkerchief, removing a good bit of his makeup. His knees were quivering.

"Relax," I told him. "Think about the money you're getting."

He grinned. "That helps."

Forrester's voice boomed in again. "Ten seconds. Places. Luck, Paul."

I didn't bother to respond, Forrester couldn't hear me anyway. Chasfield and I walked onto the stage behind the closed curtain and stood on our tape markings. The backstage lights flicked to signal that the cameras were rolling again, just as the last of the crew headed off stage and into the wings.

Through the heavy curtains I could hear Mitch Michaelson, the comedian who'd been drafted to fill the master of ceremonies position, welcoming the audience back from the commercial.

"We're very excited to have our next guest here this evening," Michaelson announced in his fine bass voice. "For those of us old enough to remember his father, Paul Galliard certainly needs no introduction. And after tonight, let's just hope he doesn't need embalming!"

It wasn't funny and nobody in the audience laughed. Through the curtains I heard Michaelson cough a few times. Then he said, "Well, I guess we should bring him out." On that abrupt note, the curtains parted. There had been no cue to applaud, so the audience and I stared at each other in dead silence. I didn't even get the polite applause accorded to after-dinner speakers.

I cleared my throat and took three steps forward. I hadn't prepared any patter, trusting to my quick wits to carry me along. I cleared my throat again. "Ladies and gentlemen," I began wittily, "this evening I will attempt to present a trick that has claimed the lives of twelve of my fellow conjurers, among them Madame DeLinsky in 1820, Professor Adam Epstein in 1869, Michael Hatal in 1899, Chung Ling Soo in 1918, and Thomas Galliard in 1959. Their deaths attest to the dangers of this effect. I perform it here tonight not to challenge death, but to honor those who have died."

I turned to Chasfield. "In a moment Lieutenant Harvey Chasfield of the New York Police Department will fire a marked bullet from the rifle you see in his hands. The bullet will travel across the stage, achieving a velocity of 3,140 feet per second, and shatter the glass panel you see behind me. The bullet will reach me shortly thereafter. I will either catch it between my teeth or die."

The audience started to come to life. I walked over to Chasfield and held out the bullet on a small china plate. "The lieutenant will now use a sharp metal point to scratch identifying marks on the bullet, so that there can be no possibility of a switch or other trickery." I held the bullet

**190**

steady on the plate while Chasfield made a few jagged lines. I could hear some excited murmuring in the crowd now. I walked toward the camera and held the bullet up to display the markings.

"Now, Lieutenant, if you would be so kind as to load the gun." As Chasfield came forward, I tilted the china plate forward slightly so that the bullet slipped through his fingers and fell to the stage. He grinned and stooped to pick it up, bobbling it a couple of times. As he tried to load the rifle, the bullet slipped from his fingers a second time.

He grinned weakly. "I'm a little nervous, I guess," he said. The audience laughed, sounding a little nervous themselves. Graciously, I retrieved the bullet and snapped it into the chamber while Chasfield held the rifle steady. The lieutenant thanked me. I smiled to indicate that it had been no trouble.

"I will now take my position behind the glass panel," I told the audience. "As you can see, the glass has been marked to assist Lieutenant Chasfield in taking aim." My eyes drifted to the cameras as I walked across to the other side of the stage. Two of them were tilted downward. Only the third, positioned directly at center stage, was in use. I couldn't help smiling. Forrester had been listening after all.

I stood on my tape mark behind the glass panel. "These plastic goggles and padded leather gloves will protect my eyes and face from flying glass," I told the camera. The gloves were bulky. I had to use my teeth to help pull on the second one.

The audience had fallen silent now, as if on cue. It was going better than I'd hoped. Earlier, Forrester had suggested that I make some kind of appeal for guidance to the spirits of my illustrious predecessors, but I had counseled restraint. Judging by the silence beyond the cameras, I was getting the desired response anyway. Also, I hadn't wanted to give a speech with a bullet in my mouth. I nodded to Michaelson to give the firing commands.

The emcee had been standing off to the side of the stage, out of camera range. Now he cleared his throat a few times and stepped forward. He looked anxious. Either that or he should have been an actor rather than a comedian.

"Are you set?" he asked.

I nodded again as the camera dollied in close.

"*Ready*," Michaelson called, his deep voice rumbling across the stage.

Through the glass I watched Chasfield shoulder the rifle.

"*Aim*."

I raised my gloved hands and braced my legs as Chasfield drew his bead. Michaelson held the moment just long enough.

"*Fire!*" he shouted.

The rifle flashed and the glass cobwebbed at the same instant. I reeled backward, grabbing a handful of the black fly curtain and jerking it down on top of me as I fell to the stage. Only then did I become aware of the sound of the rifle blast.

For a fraction of a second the entire studio was silent except for the echo of the gunshot. Then all hell broke loose. I could hear Henry's shouts above the others.

"My God!" he cried. "He's been shot!"

Happily, I wasn't shot. I saw no reason to share the glad news with the world just yet, though. I lay still under the fallen black curtain, listening to the sounds of growing pandemonium. I could feel the floorboards vibrate beneath me as people flooded the stage. It would take them a few seconds to reach me, since I'd insisted on clearing the wings before I went on. Through the folds in the curtain I could see a brightening of light. I guessed that someone had brought up the house lights.

"Someone get a doctor! Get a doctor!" cried Henry, emoting nicely.

Michaelson tried valiantly to restore order. *"Ladies and gentlemen,"* he intoned, *"please remain in your seats."*

By then the first of my rescuers had reached me. I began to stir, slowly throwing off the black curtain as though weakened by my ordeal. Chasfield and Michaelson came forward to help me, but I waved them off and struggled unsteadily to my feet. When I was certain the camera had come in tight on me, I raised my arms and triumphantly displayed the bullet clenched between my teeth.

It got a nice hand. In fact, it took a good five minutes before order was restored. They never did manage to get the stage cleared for the final dance number. I found that doubly gratifying.

Half an hour later, after the rehearsal audience had dutifully filled out their comment cards and I had shaken a lot of hands and been slapped on the back a few times, Sutton Forrester cornered me at the foot of the stage.

"Thanks for warning me," he said. "Now I have no idea whether the show will time out right."

"Sorry," I said. "I thought the effect was worth it, though."

"I trust we're in for a repeat performance tonight?"

"Lightning will strike twice, yes."

"Okay. If we can get the crew to keep their heads this time, we might really have something here. I would like to rescue the part where Chasfield confirms the markings on the bullet." He made some notes on his clipboard. "I may even lay in a few professional screamers. Just to get the shock level back up to where it was just then."

"I've already seen to that," I said.

Forrester gave a laugh. Actually, it was kind of a giggle. "Was Henry in on it?" he asked.

"Yes."

"What about you, Lieutenant?" Chasfield had wandered over to join us.

"You mean the playacting?" he asked. "I didn't know a thing about it. And Paul, for the real show? With all my buddies watching? Do you have to make me look like such a klutz?"

I handed him another bullet. "You figured it out?"

He turned the bullet over in his hand and handed it back. "Yeah, I figured it out," he said with a grin. "After only thirty years, uh?"

Forrester went back to the control room to check things over for the broadcast. Chasfield wandered off to avail himself of the studio's union-mandated buffet dinner. I headed for the wings, loosening my tie. I knew I wouldn't be able to eat.

We had slightly less than an hour until the live broadcast began. I rechecked my equipment to make sure the blast hadn't dislodged the plug I'd placed in the rifle. Then I double-checked my second prepared cartridge and replaced the shattered glass in the stand with the second pane. I also had to get my makeup redone. I'd been sweating so heavily under the studio lights that there were flesh-colored streaks on my collar. I headed back to the dressing room to change my shirt. We now had only twenty minutes to air time.

Magic Phillip had already taken his place in the parking lot with his twelve Rolls-Royces and his twenty-four show girls by the time I got back to the dressing room. I could see him in the monitor, limbering up. I noticed he'd decided on the purple T-shirt after all.

It took me three tries to get my bow tie centered. My cuff links also gave me some trouble. A knock on the door interrupted me before I could try any of the really rough stuff, like tying my shoes.

"Come in," I called.

Yen Soo Kim pushed open the door. "Please," he said. "Do I disturb?"

"Not at all," I said. "Please come in."

The Chinese magician took a few steps into the room.

194

"I came to wish luck," he said. His appearance in person was even more striking than it had been on the monitor. Yen Soo Kim had to be over six feet tall. His silken robe was imperial yellow, embroidered with a green dragon. A braided pigtail hung down his back. "Trick go well, I hope," he said.

"You're very kind," I answered. "I've admired you for many years."

He inclined his head at the compliment. "Not sure you would have heard of me."

"Of course I have. It's an honor to appear on the same bill with you. I hope to see your aerial fishing effect some day. I don't think there's anyone else in the world who still does it."

He smiled. The smile looked warm and oddly familiar. "Not difficult," he said. "I show you some day."

I motioned to a chair, but he shook his head. "Only came to wish luck," he said. "Must get ready." He took a few shuffling steps toward the door. I noticed he even wore silk slippers. At the door he hesitated and turned, his hand resting on the doorknob. "I am glad," he said. "I am glad to meet fine young magician."

That's when it hit me, hard and fast, the way great revelations will. He must have seen it in my face. "Mr. Galliard?" he said, stumbling a bit over the name. "Are you all right?"

I sat down heavily in my chair. I couldn't take my eyes from the tall conjurer's face.

He hesitated, his hand still on the doorknob. "Well. Must go. Good luck, Mr. Galliard." He pronounced it "Gah-yard." That was a nice touch.

I stared at him, making sure. "Thanks," I said. "Thanks a lot, Dad."

# Chapter 19

I guess I expected more. From the moment I had dimly perceived the possibility that my father might still be alive, I'd imagined our reunion scene. Sometimes it took place on a high cliff overlooking a turbulent sea. Other times it happened in a crowded train station, punctuated by locomotive whistles and the conductor's boarding call. Invariably the scene ended with my father burying his face in his hands and begging for my forgiveness. Slowly, his voice choked with sobs, he would explain his reasons for abandoning me and my mother. I never got around to clarifying those reasons, but usually they had something to do with secret orders from Eisenhower. Other times it was Churchill. The whole thing usually ended when he produced some sort of pendant, worn close to his heart, with a lock of my hair in it. Also, there were many repetitions of the phrase, "My God, son . . . I never dreamed . . . I never dared hope I'd see you again."

The reality fell short. One would have thought, by his expression and posture, that I had just informed Yen Soo Kim of a spot on his robe.

The tall Chinese conjurer who was not actually Chinese but was in fact my father, long thought dead, sat down and lit a cigarette. "So," he said. "You know."

I avoided looking at his face. My composure felt like some liquid I had cupped in my bare hands. "Yes," I said, struggling with a shaky voice. "I know."

His eyes swept the room. It flashed through my mind that he might be looking for concealed microphones. Actually, he needed an ashtray. "You know everything?" he asked. The Mandarin singsong was gone now. His voice was flat and almost free of accent.

"I think so," I said.

He leaned back and exhaled some smoke. "Is that why you did the bullet catch?"

"Yes," I said. I needed something to do with my hands to keep them from shaking. I felt in my pockets for a deck of cards, but I didn't have one with me. "I knew you'd survived the bullet catch, but I couldn't be sure you were still alive. If you were, I figured—I thought, if I did the trick, the trick that had supposedly killed you, you'd hear about it, and maybe—"

"When you pulled the gloves on with your teeth, was that for my benefit?"

"I wanted you to know that I knew. It was the only means I could think of to get some kind of response out of you. I have to admit, I sure as hell didn't expect results so soon. I had no way of knowing where you were. Or who, for that matter. It never crossed my mind that you'd be in the same city, much less appearing with me on the same bill."

My father crossed his legs. His entire bearing was looser now that he'd dropped the Yen Soo Kim mannerisms. He seemed relaxed—more relaxed than I thought he had any right to be. "What tipped you off?" he asked.

"You mean just now? A fella just kind of gets a special feeling when his dead father walks into the room, you know?"

198

"I didn't mean that. How did you see through my bullet catch? I have to know. My life depends on it, you could say."

"I saw a kinescope."

Having failed to locate an ashtray, he flicked his cigarette into a metal wastebasket. "That couldn't have helped you much. The bullet catch went perfectly. Hell, you know how it's done, you just did it yourself."

He had unintentionally thrust me into a comfortable role, that of lecturer. It gave me some time to collect my wits. "On the surface the bullet catch went just as you must have planned it," I said. "You were shot dead, it was a tragedy, the end. But to my eye—" I stood up and walked to the door. He'd left it open, and it suddenly occurred to me that it should be closed. "But to my eye something didn't quite fit. You'd have no way of knowing this, but your son grew up to be quite a scholar of magic. A regular historian of legerdemain. So when I saw your bullet catch, a few things leaped out at me."

He narrowed his eyes. "You figured out that I'd jammed the breech of the rifle. That much is obvious. And you must have also figured out how I snapped the cartridge. But most magicians know how that's done. The fake death, though, that was different. That was my own innovation. How'd you get wise?"

I carefully unfolded my pocket handkerchief. Then, with great ceremony, I coughed into it. Something very like admiration, or even pride, seemed to flash across my father's face, but that may have been wishful thinking on my part.

"I'd planned to play it up big during the actual show," I said. "I had no idea you'd be watching the dress rehearsal."

He was smiling now. It looked even more familiar than before. "Pretty sharp," he said.

"Yeah, well, like they say, the fruit never falls very far from the tree. When I saw you cough on that kinescope,

**199**

I knew something was up. It was too perfect a move; the ideal misdirection. I felt almost positive you were using the handkerchief as a cover while you slipped something into your mouth. It wasn't the bullet, though. You'd already popped that into your mouth when you used your teeth to help pull on the gloves. That's how I knew the trick hadn't gone wrong in the first place. You'd plainly done all the sleight of hand correctly, or you wouldn't have made the move with the gloves. So if you already had the bullet in your mouth, what was left? Why the handkerchief bit? For a second I thought maybe you actually had something stuck in your throat. Then it hit me: a capsule. A gelatin capsule full of stage blood. The oldest magician's trick in the book combined with the oldest actor's trick in the book."

My eye fell on the monitor. The broadcast had begun. Magic Phillip was dancing around amid the Rolls-Royces. "But one thing stuck in *my* throat, Pop. You mind if I call you Pop?"

He didn't respond.

"There was just one thing I couldn't work out."

"Just one?"

"Habeas corpus."

"Oh," he said. "That."

"Right. That. It's one thing to fall down and play dead there on the stage for a couple of minutes. Maybe you even managed to have good old Red Katz keep everyone away from your poor lifeless form. But it's quite another thing to get a death certificate. You even managed a coroner's report. God, I went to your funeral. There must have been *something* in that coffin."

"It wasn't so difficult," he said, grinding out his cigarette. "Things like that were easier in those days, if you knew how to go about it. We bought a skid-row stiff, greased a few palms."

There was a tortoiseshell hairbrush sitting by the dressing room mirror. I picked it up and tapped it rapidly in my palm. "Well," I said. "This certainly is an unusual situation we find ourselves in. Things like this don't happen every day."

Maybe it was the quavery pitch of my voice. Maybe it was the frantic way I kept drumming the hairbrush against my palm. Whatever the reason, my father looked alarmed for the first time since he'd entered the room. "Paul," he said, "this must be difficult for you to understand, but—"

I cut him off. "Any regrets, Pop?"

"You have to consider—"

"You know, pangs of remorse over the wife and son you left behind?"

My father flipped his braided pigtail over his shoulder. It was a smooth, natural-looking gesture, and I doubt he realized he'd done it. "What would you have me say?" he asked. "You're someone I never met, an adult I don't know. Not even remotely. Yes, I regretted the necessity of it. I regretted giving up my life. It was a good one. But I did what I had to do."

I like to think of myself as even-tempered. In fact, I take pride in it. So I wasn't at all pleased with myself for hurling the tortoiseshell brush at the mirror with all my strength. I must have thought it would make me feel better in a brutish, virile way. It didn't. If my mother ever comes back from the dead, I'll handle it more maturely.

My father stared at the shattered mirror. "You said you knew the whole story," he said. "I just assumed you understood. Jesus Christ. You and I have a lot to talk about."

I was surprised at how tired I suddenly felt. "I think we've pretty much run out of things to talk about," I said.

"Paul, don't you get it? This was no lark. I *had* to drop out of sight. I *had* to die."

"Sure," I said wearily. "Don't worry about it."

"It was Katz, he'd gotten me involved in something—"

"The war crimes thing."

"You know about that."

201

"The others were involved. They didn't seem to feel the need to fake their own deaths."

"The others weren't involved. They barely knew what was happening. I was the lucky one, the one that Katz chose to trade for his own freedom. Katz, my old ally. My closest friend. It would have happened too. I found out just before the axe fell. I went to Katz and demanded that he clear my name, but by that time the damage had been done. He couldn't stop it, no matter how much I threatened. I found I had no choice. When I . . . died, that settled things once and for all."

"How? How did that settle things?"

"It was meant to appear that I had taken the honorable way out. Chosen suicide over disgrace." He was talking rapidly and using a lot of hand gestures to help him get it all in. "So that's why I did what I did. It wasn't pretty and it wasn't noble, but it seemed preferable to the virtual certainty of standing trial as a war criminal. Can you honestly say that you would have preferred that? Do you believe you would have done any different? Many times I've cursed him for what he did to me. On the night of the shooting, after he had served his function, I beat him within an inch of his life. I believe I would have killed him if there had been time." The more urgently he spoke, the more detached from it I felt.

"Swell," I said. "Great. But that doesn't explain this interesting new look you're sporting."

"This." He smoothed down the folds of his robe. "My very own witness relocation program." He sighed heavily and smiled, ruefully. It was my cue to smile back. I didn't. "There were some rumors in the days following the bullet catch. I knew that I was going to have to lie low for a long time. I remembered reading about a magician named Chung Ling Soo—"

"I know. I know all about him."

He nodded and made some more rapid hand movements. "The man was an American who'd spent his whole life masquerading as a Chinese. I figured I could too. For a while, anyway. I was sort of doing it in reverse. His career ended with a bullet catch. Mine began with one. I never intended the act to go on forever. It started out simple: makeup, a wig. A dab of spirit gum at my temples did for the eyes. But it never—it never became possible for me to drop my guard. And by the time it didn't matter any more, Yen Soo Kim had become a big success in Europe—bigger than Thomas Galliard ever was. Over the years I refined it. Learned Chinese, found a permanent dye for my skin." He touched his eyelids. "Five years ago I had implants. I left every trace of Thomas Galliard behind me."

"Every trace," I said. "So what brings you to town now, if you don't mind my asking?"

"You really don't know what's going on at all, do you?"

"Apart from the three murders? Apart from my dead father suddenly resurfacing? No. Forgive me. I guess I haven't been keeping up."

"I planned never to set foot in America again. I didn't dare. I intended to live out my life in Europe. I've never been to China either. I couldn't hope to bring this off there. I live in London, just like Chung Ling Soo did. I wouldn't have come back unless I absolutely had to."

"Don't tell me. Let me guess. You got a wild urge to drive on the right-hand side of the road."

"It's Katz. Once again. He's in some kind of trouble. Or thinks he is. I wouldn't have believed that he would dare contact me, but I suppose I shouldn't be surprised. He says somebody's trying to kill him, somebody who wants his money. He made a lot of money back then. A pile of it. He's the only man alive—besides you, I guess—who knows who I really am, and he's threatening to spill it if I don't help him. That's how he always worked. When he's in trouble, he takes everybody with him. He says—"

"Is that why you killed him?"

His face registered pure shock. "Katz is dead?"

I pulled the broken wand from my tailcoat pocket. "Ever seen one of these before?"

His voice, when he got it to work, came out as a whisper. "Where did you get that?"

"You're a hell of an actor, Pop. Go on, do the inscrutable Asian for me again. I liked that one better."

He barely heard me. For a guy who supposedly could absorb information at a glance, he seemed to be having a good bit of trouble with this latest piece. He kept repeating the words as if examining them from all angles. "Katz is dead," he said softly. "Katz is dead. But he can't be. He can't be dead."

There was a banging at the door. I made no move to answer it. I looked instead at the studio monitor. Sanderson the Great had just finished his act. That meant Yen Soo Kim was only seconds away from missing his entrance

The banging at the door grew more urgent. "Mr. Galliard?" a voice called. "Mr. Galliard?"

My father didn't even flinch. "That's you, Paul," he said.

"What is it?" I called. "Can it wait?"

The door swung inward. Mindy Kramer stuck her head in. "Are you decent? Sorry to bother you, we're looking for Yen Soo Kim. Have you seen him? We're live here and the guy's—"

"So sorry. Lost track of time." My father, who'd been born just outside of Vienna, slipped easily back into his Charlie Chan voice. His whole face had become an impassive mask once again. I envied the gift. I certainly hadn't inherited it. "I coming now," he said. He stood up, straightened his robes, and headed toward the door. "Mr. Gah-yard," he said, turning to me, "we talk later. Most important."

He started to continue but Mindy pulled at his arm. "You have less than one minute, Mr. Kim. Come *on*." She glanced at me as she hurried him through the door. "Can you believe this guy?" she asked.

I could only shake my head.

# Chapter 20

I got only four blocks away before I told the cab driver to turn around. There didn't seem much point in throwing my career away. I don't know where I thought I was going anyway.

Magic Phillip was relaxing in the dressing room when I got back, his cheeks still flushed with the effort of vanishing twelve Rolls-Royces. "Did you catch my act?" he asked when I pushed open the door. "How was I? Did it go all right?"

"I missed it," I said. "Sorry."

"Oh. That's okay. Here, I'll get out of your way. You must need to get ready. Somebody broke our mirror, though."

"That was me. It was an accident."

"Yeah? I hope you're not superstitious." He held out a hand mirror. "You can borrow mine if you want."

My hands shook as I took it from him. "Thanks," I said. "I really am sorry I missed your act."

"Don't worry about it, Dude." He glanced at my hands. "Still nervous about the big trick? Don't worry. It was hot in dress rehearsal."

"I'll be all right," I said.

"Sure you will," said Magic Phillip. "You'll be magical." He turned to watch the studio monitor. Yen Soo Kim was halfway through the Silken Rhapsody. He didn't look nearly as polished as he had in rehearsal. His movements had a tentative quality. Magic Phillip didn't seem to notice. "You were right about this guy," he said. "He's major league."

"That man is my father," I said.

"You break me up," Magic Phillip said.

"No, really. Honestly. That man is my father."

He laughed. "You're too much!"

Mindy Kramer reappeared in the open doorway to escort me on the long walk to the stage. "Time to go," she said. "Merlini comes on next, then you. Are you set?"

"I'm set. See you later, Magic."

"Good luck, Dude. Maybe you, me, and your father could grab a burger later, what do you say?"

"I'll ask him."

Mindy led me down the narrow corridor. Already the exodus of nonessential crew members had begun, and we found ourselves bucking a heavy flow of traffic.

"Chip asked me to tell you to hold the bullet in your teeth until you're absolutely sure the camera's got it," Mindy said, more or less carrying me along the corridor. "Then let Lieutenant Chasfield confirm the scratch marks. We'll have to sort of play that by ear, since we didn't get to it in dress rehearsal."

I didn't respond. I had my eyes fixed on Yen Soo Kim, who was hurrying toward me from the opposite direction. "Mr. Gah-yard," he called. "Must speak to you." He rushed up and grabbed me by the arm.

"Sorry, we have to keep moving," Mindy said. "This is live television here."

"Just a damn minute, lady." My father had dropped the dialect.

I stopped, the three of us bottlenecking the traffic in the hallway.

"Paul, you have to tell me everything that's happened."
In his urgency, my father couldn't seem to settle on an
accent. What came out sounded vaguely French. "Where
did you get that wand? You'd better tell me everything,
so—"

"Let's keep it movin'!" called a stagehand who was
holding up the front end of a scenery panel. "You're holdin' people up here!"

My father had taken hold of both my arms. "What
happened to Katz? What happened?"

Mindy thrust her stopwatch in my face. "Paul, you
have to get on stage. We don't have much time."

"You're holdin' up progress back here!"

"Paul—son—this is urgent. We have to—"

"I'm sorry, Paul, but you're due on stage in two minutes and thirty-five seconds." Mindy pulled me away.

My father's voice trailed me down the corridor. "Come
back, son!" he called, his voice cracking. "Come back!"

Mindy tightened her grip on my arm as she tugged
me along. "That's kind of sweet, isn't it?" she asked. "He's
worried about you."

Others in the crowded passageway thought so too. A
few of them even applauded.


Things were moving a little too fast for the likes of
me. I needed time to organize my thoughts. I'm a me-
thodical person at heart. I used to meditate for an hour
before outlining a term paper. The prospect of going on
live television in two minutes did little to help matters.

Merlini had just finished when I reached the backstage
area. After a brief teaser from emcee Mitch Michaelson,
the program broke away for commercials.

Chasfield stood waiting for me. I took the rifle from
his hands and looked it over one last time. I felt in my
pocket for the bullet. Everything checked out.

Working with practiced efficiency, the stagehands
pulled down Merlini's set, rolled his Floating Lady appa-

ratus into the wings, and set my glass panel at center stage. They completed the operation in less than a minute. Chasfield and I walked onto the stage behind the closed curtains, took our marks and waited. The lieutenant wiped his forehead with his handkerchief. He looked terrible. I could only imagine how I seemed to him.

Through the heavy curtains I heard Michaelson begin my introduction. He'd thought up a new joke during the dinner break, and it went over better with the crowd. The curtains parted and I stepped forward to a round of warm applause.

Later, friends would call to say that I had been quite good on the program. Eventually I sat down to watch it on videotape, and I must allow that I did passably well. But if anyone looked closely, my distraction was plain to see. My eyes met the camera, but never really made contact. I might as well have been staring off into space.

My speech about the history of the bullet catch had the desired effect, and the audience had begun its stirrings and rumblings in earnest by the time Chasfield came forward to mark the bullet. I only made him drop the bullet once this time, so that I could retrieve it and load the gun. I suspect he might have dropped the bullet anyway, even if I hadn't coated it with machine oil. His hands were so damp that he'd had to blot them with his handkerchief.

I crossed the stage and took my mark behind the glass panel. Something Schneider had said echoed through my mind as I pulled on my gloves and protective goggles. Something about the private, unseen magic that occurs during each effect. Michaelson stepped forward at my nod to begin the countdown. It dawned on me then that the unseen magic had passed me by this time.

Over Chasfield's shoulder I saw a knot of crew members and technicians watching from the wings. They shouldn't have been there. The area was supposed to have been cleared. Someone approached them from behind whom I didn't recognize. He wore a hat and dark glasses.

That seemed odd to me. So did the fact that he continued walking toward the stage, skirting the people standing behind the scenes as if about to make an entrance.

*"Ready."*

Once more Michaelson's deep voice rumbled across the stage. Chasfield shouldered the rifle, oblivious to the approach from behind of the man in the dark glasses.

*"Aim."*

Chasfield sighted along the barrel. So did the man in the dark glasses. He had a revolver in his outstretched hand. A thirty-eight, by the look of it.

I like to tell myself that I figured it out just then, that all the pieces fell into place and I clearly foresaw the consequences. In truth I had only the broad outlines. All I knew for sure was that there were two guns pointed at me now and that I didn't like the looks of either of them.

I threw myself backward just as the revolver went off. The shot hit Chasfield in the back and drove him to his knees. The man in the dark glasses continued forward without breaking stride, firing a second shot as he emerged from the wings and a third as he stepped into full audience view.

By that time Chasfield had already squeezed his trigger. In dress rehearsal the shot had appeared to punch a dramatic hole in the glass. Now, the entire pane of glass and half the metal stand disappeared in a spray. I saw it happen from the stage floor. Instinct told me to shield my eyes, but it was just as well that I had the goggles. Only one arm would move.

*"Ladies and gentlemen. Please remain in your seats!"* Michaelson's voice had risen an octave. *"Do not panic!"*

I heard screams. Some of them may have been mine. Chasfield was on his face, his arms were straight out over his head, still clutching the rifle. The man in the hat and dark glasses stood over him. He may have been checking to be sure Chasfield was dead, but I couldn't be certain.

*"If you would please remain in your seats, ladies and gentlemen—"*

I could feel heat. A lot of heat. I looked down. A dark stain was spreading across the stage.

The crowd noise nearly deafened me now. People were rushing toward me, but I wasn't interested in them. I tried to keep my eyes focused on the retreating figure with the hat, but I kept losing him. People's legs were in the way.

Someone propped my head up. That's when the pain hit. It's funny what you think about at a moment like that. My thoughts weren't of the dead man lying a few feet away. They weren't of the man in the hat and dark glasses. They weren't even about the bullet that had been fired from the Nitro Express. Lying there on the stage, bleeding and in pain, I thought about the trick. The trick that had gone wrong.

# Chapter 21

It was a bicycle chain this time. The chain had slipped its gears and gotten grease all over Bobby's favorite corduroy pants. Cheryl, reprising her role as the beleaguered housewife, seemed pretty much at her wit's end. "I don't think this stain will *ever* come out," she said, wailing a little.

I leaned into frame through the doorway of the laundry room. "Having trouble with those persistent grease stains?" I asked. "Hi, I'm Paul Galliard, and I recommend—"

Cheryl's face told me I'd screwed it up.

"What?" I asked. "What? I said 'persistent.' Not 'pesky.' I swear it."

Terry's voice boomed in through the studio speaker. "It's the cast, Paul. You leaned too far in. We can see the cast under your cape."

I looked down at the white plaster encasing my right arm. "Sorry," I said.

"No problem. Let's try wrapping the cape around the cast a little more securely."

We got the segment in two more takes, and I wandered

into the control room while Cheryl taped some reaction shots. Wade Judson lowered himself into the seat next to me. "How you feeling?" he asked.

"Stiff. Other than that, no problems. I'm going to be wearing this thing for two months, though."

"I wanna thank you for coming back, you know, with your wing in a sling and everything. Especially since I know you must be getting some big offers now, with all the publicity over what happened."

"I appreciate all you've done for me, Wade. You've been more than generous, especially with your insurance benefits."

He grinned. "Sales are up. Way up. I can afford to be generous. And who knew when we signed you that you'd get us so much free publicity?"

I looked through the glass at the studio clock. It was time for a pain pill. "Listen, Wade, I have to get some water. I'll be back in a few minutes."

"Take your time. I don't think Terry needs you for another hour or so."

I headed out of the studio into the adjoining hallway. I filled a paper cup with water from the cooler and swallowed a pill. While I waited for it to work I sat down on a padded bench and closed my eyes. My arm hurt like hell. I wiggled my fingers and thought about the indignity of it all. I hadn't even been hit by a bullet, just shards of glass. There'd been plenty of damage, though. Nerves. Tendons. I wiggled my fingers some more and wondered how long it would take for full movement to return. The surgeon hadn't been able to tell me whether or not I'd ever regain the full dexterity of my right hand. Therapy can work miracles, he'd said. I could, too, at one time, I thought.

I felt a tap on my good shoulder. "Private daydream?"

I opened my eyes. Clara sat down next to me on the bench. "I heard you were in the building," she said. "I've been watching the hallway, hoping you'd come out of there. How are you feeling?"

"Like a wounded sparrow," I said. "Like a tiny, fragile sparrow with one of its precious wings—"

"Galliard, you said you were going to rest up. You said no work for at least three weeks. This is only one week."

"Yes, well, this isn't really work. And besides, I got a little restless holed up all alone, sorting through the letters of concern, fielding offers from agents, ducking reporters. Luckily I had plenty to read. Tell Franklin I very much enjoyed the coloring book."

"Have you seen the latest?" She held up one of the city's gaudier tabloids. A headline read MAGIC GUNMAN STILL AT LARGE.

" 'Magic gunman,' " I said. "I kind of like that."

She folded back the page and scanned the article. I watched her out of the corner of my eye. "They're basically recycling the same story," she said, a little too casually. "It's been that way all week."

"Slow news week, you suppose?"

"Not especially. I guess people are just still interested in what happened. They want to hear about it."

"Imagine," I said.

I'd seen Clara every day since the shooting and she hadn't once asked me for the details. I knew it was killing her.

"I mean, there haven't been any new developments," she continued. "Except for the police board of inquiry, and lord knows that could drag on for months. I don't know why everyone keeps going on about it. Over on my program, they've replayed the footage almost every day. They keep finding some fresh reason to justify showing it again: your release from the hospital, Chasfield's funeral . . ."

"I guess it is a big story," I said.

"I guess it is," she said. "A big story, I mean." She chewed at her lip.

I decided to end her misery. "Okay," I said. "Let's go."

"Where?"

"You're going to buy me a cup of coffee and I'm going

to hand you my exclusive, backstage report on the affair of the magic gunman."

"You mean it?"

"Of course I mean it. How long were you going to hold out before you asked me?"

"Forever. I swear. I didn't want to take advantage, you know, I didn't want to presume on our relationship to get the story, even though it would only be about the biggest break I ever got and could mean a promotion to on-air for me. But you haven't said a word, and I assumed you didn't want to talk about it or you would have said something by now."

"It's fine. I'll talk. Let's get that coffee."

She didn't seem to hear me about the coffee. "Wait right here a minute," she said. "I'll be right back." She vanished down the hallway, returning a moment later with an interview recorder. "You're sure it's all right?" she asked.

"Yes," I said. "Honest. I have a desperate need to cleanse my soul."

"Not here. Follow me." She took my good arm and led me to the equipment storage room where we'd watched the kinescope. "You won't have to pick the lock this time. I got the right key." She unlocked the door and led me down the half flight of steps into the storage area.

"This is very cozy," I said, "but why here?"

"You're a hot commodity, bud. I have to protect my story."

"There's a lot of that in my business too." I sat down on a wood-topped stool.

"You ready?"

"Sure," I said. "Shoot. Or rather, ask away."

She set the tape recorder on a stool between us and clicked it on. "The papers are all saying that Lieutenant Chasfield was leaning on your friend Katz pretty hard," she said, taking care to speak clearly. "The police department has clamped down tight on it, so I have to believe

**214**

there's some truth to it. Call it whatever you want—black-mail, extortion, protection—it seems Katz turned over a lot of money to Chasfield during the last three months. Katz's records show it. Nobody's turned any of it up on Chasfield's end yet, though."

"Chasfield would have hidden it pretty well."

"Well, the question of the hour is, what hold did Chasfield have over Katz? Katz was a model citizen. He had a distinguished-services record a mile long. He came out of World War Two a real hero."

"I'm glad to have that confirmed," I said.

"I did some digging and found out that Katz made his money a long time ago. During the fifties. But as far as I can tell, his only job at the time was managing your father and the other magicians. It doesn't follow that that made him rich."

"It sure doesn't," I agreed.

"Which brings us to the rumors of profiteering. Any truth to that?"

I nodded. She jerked her head at the tape recorder. I cleared my throat. "I believe those rumors are true, Miss Bidwell," I said.

"And that's what Chasfield was using to blackmail him?"

"It was more than just that."

"More?"

I used my good arm to shift the cast so the weight rested on my leg. I hadn't been able to wear the sling with my costume. "Did you see yesterday's headlines?" I asked.

"Which one? 'It Was Horrible, Cries Witness'?"

"The other one. 'Arrow Victim Had Nazi Ties.' "

"That was true?"

"I can't tell you for sure. I hope not. Clément says it's not true, but he seems to have been in the dark about a lot of what was going on. All I can tell you with any certainty is that Katz wasn't too particular about who he did business with."

"These Nazi ties, did they have anything to do with the killings?"

"The Gestapo wasn't involved, if that's what you mean."

"That wasn't what I meant and you know it."

"Look. Katz wasn't a Nazi. I really believe that. But his hands were dirty and the Nazi hunters were interested in him. Chasfield knew that."

"But if Chasfield wanted to blackmail Katz, why wait all these years? It happened so long ago."

"I couldn't tell you."

"Try."

"Well, I've had a lot of time to think about this over the past few days. A lot of time." I couldn't get comfortable on the stool. I got up and tried resting the cast on a storage shelf. Clara followed me with the tape recorder. "Chasfield only got drawn in because he was a good marksman. At the time, he couldn't have had any idea what was going on behind the scenes. But the shooting changed his life. He told me so the other night in his office. I have some sympathy for that. At first I think he must have held himself responsible for what had happened. Later, when he began to put things together, he must have started feeling like a victim. After all, this one piece of bad luck, which wasn't even his fault, had ruined his life. Thwarted his chances for advancement. Excited talk among his friends. I think when word of the *Cavalcade* reunion came around, he saw an opportunity to make things right."

"By killing everyone who'd been on the original program."

"Hardly. Chasfield wasn't crazy." The shelf idea wasn't working, so I crossed the room and sat down on the half flight of stairs, resting my arm on the next step up. Again Clara followed with the tape recorder. "I doubt if Chasfield planned to kill anyone at first. I think he just wanted money. As much as he could get. So he threatened Katz. He even got creative about it, using one of the magic wands he'd walked off with on the night of the shooting."

"What do you mean, *one* of the wands? He sent those things all over town."

"Yeah, but I doubt if Chasfield ever intended to involve Schneider or Nussbaum when he began blackmailing Katz. He was after money, and neither of them had any."

"So how did the others get into it?"

"Katz roped them in, trying to save himself. That was how he worked. Strength in numbers. Maybe he hoped Chasfield would back down if the others were involved, but it only wound up raising the stakes."

"How's that?"

"When Chasfield tried putting pressure on the others, the whole thing blew up. After all, Schneider, Nussbaum, and Clément were fairly clean. And they didn't owe any great loyalty to Red Katz. In fact, Clément wasn't even sure he was still alive until a few days ago. So the three of them weren't afraid to make noise, or go to the police if necessary. Obviously that made them a problem for Lieutenant Chasfield."

"So he killed them?"

"After the threats failed, yes."

"You mean the wands."

"Right, the wands. Chasfield must have hoped he could scare them off. Like I said, I don't think he had any strong desire to kill anyone."

Clara peered down at the recorder to check how much tape she had left. "He sure turned out to be good at it, though. Killing people, I mean."

"The man was a homicide detective. Like he said to me, he'd seen it all, twice. Nussbaum mentioned right before he died that he tested out his dove act at a public library show a few days earlier. Schneider used to do the same thing all the time. That must have been where Chasfield set things up. You know, poisoned Schneider's balloons, diddled with Nussbaum's flashpot. I've done some library shows myself. If anyone had wanted to tamper with my equipment, it would have been simple enough. There's always some lag between story time and the magic show."

I looked at my watch. The Stain Begone people would start missing me soon. "Killing Schneider and Nussbaum pretty much ensured that they wouldn't go to the police. It also kept Clément fairly quiet, and it increased the pressure on Katz to fork over the money."

"But Katz got killed too."

"So he did. But not with one of those fatal magic effects. And a pistol crossbow isn't the sort of thing Chasfield would have owned or had access to. I double-checked that with Michael. It was something the OSS developed for its quiet killing. That puts it more in Katz's line."

"I'm not sure how the crossbow thing fits, then."

"It doesn't, unless you figure me into it."

"Oh really? Did you kill somebody too? This is getting to be an even better interview than I bargained for."

"Why do you suppose Katz invited me out to Grant's Tomb that night? It wasn't because he had some important piece of news to share with me, although I thought so at the time. He wanted me involved, just like he'd involved Schneider and Nussbaum, whether I wanted to be or not. When Clément called to say that I wanted to meet with him, Katz must have seen an opportunity to wedge someone else between himself and Chasfield. If he arranged a meeting—to make a payment, say—and I showed up, there'd be one more person sharing the dirty secret. The news of my impending arrival would have delighted the lieutenant. He'd already had to set the fire in my apartment to cover his tracks after Schneider's death, so—"

"He didn't have to set that fire," Clara said. "He could have just stolen the balloons."

"The fire was for intimidation, like the broken wands. It was no coincidence that explosion happened right when I walked through the door of my apartment. Chasfield had it rigged to go off at the ringing of the phone. He must have been down on the street watching me go in the building, and then called my number from the pay phone on the corner. Lucky for him it was working. All Chasfield wanted was for everyone to clear off and let him blackmail Katz in his own quiet way. Katz pushed it too hard the night he died. Even then, I doubt if Chasfield intended to kill him. Maybe he just started to work him over a little. Katz had a black eye. And I'll bet Katz, the old war hero, decided to do something about it with his pistol crossbow."

"And Chasfield got it away from him."

"All we know is that Katz got an arrow in his skull. It explains a lot, though. Like why Giunt and his friends didn't see anyone but me come out of the tomb that night. All Chasfield had to do was stay inside until the police arrived, then mingle in with them. Most natural thing in the world. An old magician's trick: hiding in plain sight."

"Chasfield seems to have known a great deal about magic. Schneider and Nussbaum's deaths had you thinking a magician was involved."

"He'd been stewing for thirty years over what happened on the *Magic Cavalcade* broadcast. You can learn a lot about anything in that amount of time. He must have read up on bullet catches through the ages. He'd learned well. I saw him do a trick in the last minutes of his life."

"What was that?"

"It had to do with a handkerchief. A lot of them do. Backstage before the broadcast I double-checked to make sure the rifle was ready. When I handed it back to Chasfield, he had a handkerchief in his hands. He'd been wiping his forehead with it."

"I don't see—"

"You wouldn't. I should have. He kept the handkerchief with him on stage. He kept wiping his hands with it. When I bent down to pick up the dropped shell, he used the handkerchief as a cover while he slipped another slug into the breech. Not an entire shell, just the slug. He'd moved my rubber stopper just slightly so the bullet would fit but I wouldn't notice the change. That way, when the blank went into the gun during the broadcast, it fit snugly into place behind the second slug. In effect, two halves of two different bullets came together in the gun. When I put in my blank charge, it was as if I actually loaded the gun."

"Why didn't he just kill you when you showed up at Grant's Tomb, since he obviously planned to do it anyway the next night?"

"His great affection for me must have prevented it."

"Seriously."

"I don't think he really did plan to kill me. Not then, anyway. A few hours later I made the mistake of telling him what I knew about Katz's past."

She pushed back a handful of her hair as if that might help her think. Maybe it did. "In other words, you made a slip. You let Chasfield know that you knew what he'd been using to twist Katz's arm?"

"Right. Only I didn't know that he'd been twisting anybody's arm at the time."

"He must have thought you'd figure it out eventually."

"I did figure it out eventually."

"A little late."

"Very much too late." I glanced down at Clara's interview recorder, watching the tape counter turn. I hoped I'd given her a good story, but it sure wasn't the whole story. Chasfield had figured it out, all right. Everything. He knew that my father had survived. He must have. Chasfield had been chosen to participate in the original broadcast because of his prowess with guns. A marksman would know the difference between firing a blank and a real bullet. He'd also know what a round of that caliber would do to a man. He'd been in position to see the bullet hit. Somewhere along the line he must have put it all together. When I pulled the same stunt in dress rehearsal, Chasfield would have known he'd have to kill me. The one thing he hadn't counted on was that the only other man who knew the whole story would be standing right behind him with a thirty-eight revolver.

Clara looked over at me. "You know that still leaves me with one question. A biggie."

I kept quiet.

"You know what it is."

I examined my feet.

"Who was the guy in the hat and the dark glasses?"

"I don't know," I said, "but I sure would like to thank him."

"I think you do know. I think you're perfectly well aware who the magic gunman is, and you're keeping quiet about it because you think you owe him your life."

"Call me sentimental."

"For a while I thought it might have been your friend Clément, avenging his buddies, but then I watched the videotape. Several times. Whoever it was was a good foot taller than Clément."

"The guy had to be almost as tall as I am."

"You do know, don't you." We locked eyes. Would she have believed me if I told her who the magic gunman was? Would she have believed me if I told her that after the shooting he simply changed back into Yen Soo Kim, the Asian Astonisher? Later that night, with the help of an interpreter, he had calmly answered questions for the police, though they didn't find him of much use. By the time I got out of the hospital, he had left the country.

"I guess that does it," Clara said, turning off the tape recorder. "Thank you. Really."

"The pleasure was all mine."

"Can I give you a ride home later?"

"Thank you."

We walked up the stairs and Clara held the door open for me. "Paul, what are you going to do until your arm heals?"

"I don't know. I might travel. It'd be good to get out of town for a while, let the whole thing blow over."

"What if—what if your arm doesn't heal? What will you do then?"

I looked down at the cast. "It's horrible to think about, but I might have to get a job."

# Chapter 22

The prodding in my ribs got my attention. I turned my head away from the window.

"Were you asleep?" asked the girl with the stuffed walrus.

"You mean because it's the middle of the night and I was sitting here with my eyes closed, snoring?"

"You weren't snoring," she said. "I would have heard you. You were looking out the window."

"I'm a very quiet snorer. I've been in training for years."

She looked at the vacant seat next to me. "Is this seat taken?" she asked.

"No," I said. "It most certainly isn't taken."

"May I sit down? Just for a moment?"

"Please do. Forgive me for not standing. I haven't yet learned how to get out of this seat belt."

"You just lift up on the metal buckle," she said, sliding into the seat next to me. "Like the lady said at the beginning."

"I must not have been paying attention. Are you traveling alone?"

"No. My parents and my stupid brother are back there. You're the magician, aren't you? I've seen you."

"That is correct. I am *the* magician. You've put it beautifully. Do you have business in London, may I ask?"

"We're on vacation."

"We must be past Iceland by now. From here on in you must say that you're on holiday. The Londoners will expect it. Who's your friend?"

She held out the stuffed walrus for my inspection. "Miss Withers," she said. "She's a walrus."

"I can see that."

"She eats fish."

"A lot of fish?"

"Pretty much. How did you hurt your arm?"

With my left arm I moved my right arm off the hand rest. The smaller cast made it possible to travel, but it was still awkward as hell. "A walrus bit me," I said.

"Sure."

"What's your name?"

"Margaret. Can you show me a trick?"

"I don't know if I can. My arm makes it sort of difficult."

"Don't you know any one-arm tricks? I could go back to my seat and get a deck of cards. The lady gave them to us when we took off."

"That's all right. I have some cards." I reached into my pocket with my good arm and pulled out my blue Fan Backs. "You're going to have to bear with me here, Margaret. This may not measure up to the high standards of *the* magician. . . ."

"I bet it'll be good."

"Your confidence inspires me. Pick a card, any card." I managed a one-handed thumb fan. "Now look at it, but don't let me see what it is."

"Did you see?"

"No. Now put it back in the deck."

"Are you sure you didn't see it?"

"Honest. Now I want you to take the cards and carefully put them back in the box, all right? Leave the top open."

"Like this?"

"Exactly like that." I dipped into my inside breast pocket.

"That's a magic wand, isn't it?" Margaret asked.

"Why, yes. Now that you mention it. It is a magic wand."

"My brother has a magic wand, but not like that. His is just plastic. It doesn't do anything."

"Mine does a great deal. Watch. I wave it over the cards and look what happens, a card rises out of the pack! That wouldn't be the one you chose, would it?"

"Yeah, it is. You peeked."

"I'm working with a handicap, Margaret."

"It's still a pretty good trick, though. With the card coming up."

"You're very kind to say so."

"I bet the wand does it."

"You may be right."

"It looks old."

"The wand? It is old, but I only got it a few days ago. It came in the mail. You might say that's why I'm making this trip. I want to find the person who sent it to me."

"What for?"

"I'm not exactly sure."

"That's not a very good reason to take a trip all the way across the ocean."

"It's the only one I have."

"Could you show me another trick? Show me a lot of tricks, but don't show any to my brother. He's—"

A sleepy-looking woman appeared in the aisle. "Margaret, you're bothering this man. Come back to your seat."

"I'm not bothering him. He's only sitting here."

"Back to your seat. Now."

"Okay."

The woman smiled apologetically at me. "I'm sorry if she was bothering you."

"She wasn't, so don't be," I said. "Enjoy your vacation, Margaret."

"I'm not on vacation," she said, heading down the aisle. "I'm on holiday."